Who's Been Sleeping in My Grave?

Zach Pepper's teacher is away for the rest of the school year. Yes! Zach thinks. Party time! Until he meets his substitute teacher, Miss Gaunt, a lonely ghost who's looking for a little company—in her grave!

Stay Away from the Tree House

Dylan and Steve were happy to move to Fear Street. They finally had a backyard. And trees! And a tree house! They were happy—until they found out that their tree house was haunted!

Fright Knight

Have you met Sir Thomas Barlayne? Mike Conway has. The evil spirit lives in a haunted suit of armor that's downstairs in Mike's dad's museum! Can Mike survive a duel to the death

Also from R.L. Stine

The Beast®
The Beast® 2

R.L. Stine's Ghosts of Fear Street

Available from MINSTREL Books

R·L·STINE'S
GHOSTS OF FEARSTREET®

CREEPY COLLECTION #1:
HAPPY HAUNTINGS!

A Parachute Book

A MINSTREL® BOOK

Published by POCKET BOOKS
New York   London   Toronto   Sydney   Tokyo   Singapore

This book consists of works of fiction. Names, characters, places and incidents are products of the authors' imaginations or are used fictitiously. Any resemblance to actual events or locales or persons, living or dead, is entirely coincidental.

These titles were previously published individually.

 A Minstrel Paperback published by
POCKET BOOKS, a division of Simon & Schuster Inc.
1230 Avenue of the Americas, New York, NY 10020

Who's Been Sleeping in My Grave? copyright © 1995 by Parachute Press, Inc.
Stay Away from the Tree House copyright © 1996 by Parachute Press, Inc.
Fright Knight copyright © 1996 by Parachute Press, Inc.

WHO'S BEEN SLEEPING IN MY GRAVE? WRITTEN BY STEPHEN ROOS
STAY AWAY FROM THE TREE HOUSE WRITTEN BY LISA EISENBERG
FRIGHT KNIGHT WRITTEN BY CONNIE LAUX

ISBN: 0-671-02292-X

First Minstrel Books paperback printing February 1998

10 9 8 7 6 5 4 3 2 1

FEAR STREET is a registered trademark of Parachute Press, Inc.

A MINSTREL BOOK and colophon are registered trademarks of Simon & Schuster Inc.

Printed in the U.S.A.

GHOSTS of FEAR STREET®

WHO'S BEEN SLEEPING IN MY GRAVE?

Believe me, it isn't easy walking to school with your nose stuck in a book. In two blocks I had already tripped over a curb and bumped into a mailbox.

But I had to finish *Power Kids!*

"The sooner you read it, the sooner you'll be free from terror forever," the cover claimed. And if you know Shadyside, you know why I *needed* to finish the book—fast.

In regular towns you worry about regular things.

In Shadyside you worry about ghosts.

At least I do.

I'm scared of the ghost who wants to play hide-and-seek with kids in the Fear Street woods. I've never seen it myself. But I know people who have.

I'm scared of the burned-out Fear Street mansion. Ghosts have lived there for years and years. At least that's what my friends in school tell me.

And I have nightmares about Fear Street. It's the creepiest street in town—maybe in the whole world. Kevin, my fifteen-year-old brother, says the ghosts that haunt Fear Street are really evil. And horrible things will happen if they catch you.

I think Kevin is really evil. He loves trying to scare me.

But he won't be able to—not after I finish *Power Kids!* Nothing will scare me then. The book guarantees it—or I get my money back.

The kids in my class are going to be pretty upset. They love scaring me, too. Especially on Halloween—which is this Friday, only five days away.

Last Halloween they convinced me that a ghost salesman ran the shoe section in Dalby's Department Store. So I wore high-tops with huge holes in them all winter long. My toes froze.

Sometimes I imagine my friends keeping score. Whoever comes up with the story that scares me the most wins.

I hate it! But I'm almost a Power Kid now. So they'll have to find a new game this Halloween.

"Hey, Zack!" someone yelled.

I didn't bother to glance up from my book. It was Chris Hassler—one of my friends from school.

Chris and I are really different. Chris is short and chubby. He has bright red, curly hair and lots of freckles. Chris is usually laughing—or seems as if he's about to.

I do not look as if I'm about to burst out laughing. Big surprise, right? My grandmother says I have "very serious" eyes, like all the men in the Pepper family.

I have straight brown hair and I'm much taller than Chris. In fact, I'm the tallest kid in the fifth grade.

"Hey, Zack, wait up!" Chris called.

I kept my eyes glued to *Power Kids!* and walked faster.

Chris grabbed my arm as I hurried by his front gate. "Didn't you hear me?" he asked.

"Of course I heard you." I jerked my arm away. "I was trying to ignore you."

I crammed *Power Kids!* into my book bag as fast as I could. Chris would laugh his guts out if he spotted it.

"What are you hiding in there?" Chris demanded.

"Something my grandmother gave me for my birthday last week," I said.

"Your grandmother didn't give you any book! She gave you those polka-dot socks. I was at your party. Remember?"

"How could I forget?"

Chris grinned. "Come on. The snake I gave you was a cool present. I can't help it if you thought it was real. And you screamed your head off."

I reached into my backpack and pulled out the slimy rubber snake. "Well, it could have been real!" I shook it in his face.

Chris slapped the snake away. "If you hate it so much, how come you're carrying it around?"

"So I never forget how everyone laughed when I threw the box across the room," I explained. "Every time I see that snake, it will remind me not to let anyone scare me. Ever. Especially you." I returned the rubber snake to my backpack.

"Aw, come on, Zack," Chris whined. "Can't you take one little joke?"

"It's not one little joke," I insisted. "It's a lot of big jokes. Only they're not funny. They're mean!"

"It's not like I *tried* to be mean." Chris sounded hurt.

"Yeah, right." I snorted. "You thought I *wanted* to make a fool of myself at my own party."

"I'm sorry, Zack," he said quietly. "You're my best friend. And I really need to talk to you about something. Something serious."

"What?" I asked.

Chris slowly walked back toward his front door, his head down. He sat on the steps. I followed him.

"It's about a dog," Chris began. He talked so low I could hardly hear him. "I'm really worried about it."

"You're worried about a dog?" I said.

Chris peered left, then right. To see if anyone was listening. Then he whispered, "This isn't a regular dog. It's a ghost dog."

"A ghost dog!" I glared at Chris. "I know what you're trying to—"

"I'm not kidding this time," Chris interrupted. "I'm not. And I'm really scared."

Remember the snake, Zack, I told myself. Remember the snake. But then I noticed Chris's hands. They were trembling. Now I felt bad for being suspicious. "Okay," I said. "Tell me about it."

"Well, about a week ago we started hearing a dog howling in the middle of the night. We searched for it. But we never found it. Then last night, my dad . . ." Chris hesitated.

"What?" I demanded.

"Last night my dad was taking the garbage out. And the ghost dog lunged for him." Chris swallowed hard.

"Why do you think it's a *ghost* dog?" I asked.

Chris inhaled deeply. "Dad used the garbage can lid to shield himself—but the dog jumped right through it.

Now my hands began to tremble.

"Wh-what does the ghost dog look like?" I stammered.

"It's pure white, with a big black spot on one side," Chris replied.

"Dad's sure the dog will be back tonight. And I'm really afraid."

Chris had barely finished his sentence when we heard it.

Howling.

I jerked my head up—and there it was. Coming right at me. A white dog. With a big black spot on its side.

The ghost dog!

2

The ghost dog growled. A mean growl. Then he leaped on top of me and knocked me down. The back of my head hit the top step with a thud.

A drop of the dog's hot saliva dripped down my neck.

I squeezed my eyes shut. I'm dead meat. Dead meat.

"Here, boy!" Chris yelled.

My eyes shot wide open. Chris stood over me, hugging the ghost dog.

"Gotcha!" he cried. "This is my cousin's dog. We're keeping him while my cousin's on vacation!"

I jumped up and grabbed my backpack off the porch. I couldn't think of anything rotten enough to call Chris Hassler. So I spun around and left.

"Zack!" Chris yelled. "You're not really mad, are you?"

I slammed the gate behind me. That's it, I ordered myself. No more falling for stupid ghost stories. Not from Chris. Not from my brother, Kevin. Not from anybody.

I hurried down the street. I noticed jack-o'-lanterns on some porches. And the big oak tree near the corner of Hawthorne Street had little strips of white sheets blowing from its branches.

This Halloween nothing is going to scare me. Nothing.

Chris raced after me. "How long are you going to hold a grudge this time?" he asked, panting.

"Go away," I snapped.

We turned the corner and I spotted the back of my best friend, Marcy Novi. She was headed toward school. Marcy sits in front of me in Miss Prescott's class. Which explains why I'm so good at recognizing her from the back.

I trotted up to her. Chris followed.

"Hi, guys," Marcy said. "Zack, what happened to your jacket?" She pointed to my sleeve.

I stared down. A jagged tear ran from my wrist to my elbow.

"Zack saved my life this morning," Chris answered before I could say anything. "He's a hero."

"Really?" Marcy asked, all excited.

"Yep," Chris said. "Zack rescued me from a ghost dog."

Marcy shook her head. "Another dumb joke, huh? And you fell for it, Zack?"

I shrugged.

Marcy doesn't make fun of people. That's one of the reasons she's my best friend. She's a good listener, too. I can really talk to her when something is bugging me.

The three of us hurried up the block and into school. As we reached Miss Prescott's class, the door flew open. Debbie Steinford burst into the hallway. Debbie's the shortest girl in the class. She tries to make up for it by having the biggest hair.

"Aren't you supposed to be going in the other direction?" Marcy asked. "The bell is about to ring."

Debbie shook her head. Her hair whipped my face. "We have a substitute teacher today. She wants new chalk from the supply closet."

"What happened to Miss Prescott?" I asked.

"I don't know," Debbie answered. "Sick, I guess."

Chris grinned. "A substitute. Cool. Let's all drop our books on the floor at nine-thirty. And then—"

"No way," I interrupted.

"But that's what substitutes are for," Chris said. "Don't be such a dweeb."

"Me? A dweeb? Do you think I'm a dweeb, Marcy?" I asked.

"Well, I can't picture you giving a substitute a hard time," Marcy said. "But that doesn't make you a dweeb."

"I bet even Chris will be nice to this sub." Debbie lowered her voice. "She's creepy."

"What do you mean?" I asked. I slid my hand into my backpack and touched the rubber snake. Careful, I told myself.

"I think she's a ghost, Zack," Debbie whispered.

"What's going on?" I demanded. "Is everyone trying to get a head start on Halloween—the official Scare Zack Day? Well, forget it. It's not working."

"But the substitute does look like a ghost," Debbie insisted, her eyes growing wide. "Her skin is so white, you can practically see through it. It's totally weird."

10

"Then I can't wait to get to class." I pushed past them. "Weird is what I like from now on."

I flung open the door to our classroom.

I choked back a scream.

Our new teacher *was* a ghost.

3

The substitute didn't have a face. Only two dark spots where her eyes should be. And she hovered above the floor.

I glanced around the classroom. Why didn't any of the other kids appear to be scared?

I focused on the substitute again. A veil! She's wearing a veil. That's why I thought she didn't have a face.

And she's not floating. She's wearing a fluffy white skirt that hangs to the floor. And white shoes.

And shiny white gloves. Nothing frightening about that. Strange, yes. Scary, no.

I took a deep breath and crossed the room to my desk. I felt pretty proud of myself. I had managed not to scream. And not to run away. I had remained calm and found the explanation.

Yes! I thought. I am a Power Kid.

I watched the substitute slowly reach up and remove her hat and veil. Her face was very wrinkled. And very pale. It was almost as white as her clothes. And it seemed sort of frozen.

Her scalp showed through her thin white hair. She must be a hundred years old, I thought.

Chris, Marcy, and Debbie entered the room as the bell rang.

"Good morning, boys and girls," the substitute began. "My name is Miss Gaunt. I'll be your teacher until Miss Prescott is feeling better. She's probably going to be out for the entire week. Perhaps in art class we can make a get-well card for her. Now please stand for the Pledge of Allegiance."

As soon as we finished the pledge, Miss Gaunt reached into the top drawer of the desk for Miss Prescott's attendance book.

"Abernathy, Danny," she called in a high, trembly voice.

"Here."

"Here?" she asked as she scanned the room.

"Just here? In my day young boys and girls always addressed their elders by name."

"Here, Miss Gaunt," Danny replied.

"Oh, that's much better, Danny," she said happily.

Miss Gaunt called more names. I noticed that she took the time to say something to each kid after she checked them off in the book.

"Hassler, Christopher."

"Here, Miss Gaunt," Chris called.

"What a good, clear voice you have, Chris," Miss Gaunt commented.

She continued to read out the names. I wonder what she'll say when she gets to me?

"Novi, Marcy."

"Here, Miss Gaunt," Marcy answered.

Miss Gaunt glanced up at Marcy. "What lovely hair you have, my dear."

"Thank you, Miss Gaunt."

"Pepper, Zachariah."

"Here, Miss Gaunt," I said.

"Zachariah. Such a lovely old-fashioned name." She closed her eyes and sighed.

"Everyone calls me Zack, Miss Gaunt," I told her. "Even my mom and dad."

"But you won't mind if I call you Zachariah,

14

will you?" she asked. "You'll be making an old woman very happy, you know."

I felt my ears turn hot. They always do that when I'm embarrassed.

"Sure," I mumbled.

Chris turned around in his seat, grinning at me. And mouthing one word over and over. I didn't have to be an expert lip-reader to know the word was *dweeb*.

When Miss Gaunt finished calling roll, she strolled up and down the aisles. She seemed to be studying us.

As she walked along the last row, next to the windows, a horrible squeaking sound filled the classroom. It made my teeth ache. What is that noise? I wondered.

I glanced over to the window ledge where Homer sits. Homer is our class hamster. He was running on his treadmill. I'd never seen him move so fast. The metal wheel squeaked louder and louder as he ran faster and faster.

What's wrong with him? I thought. We named Homer after Homer Simpson because he's such a couch potato. Walking to his food dish is his total exercise.

That's probably why the wheel is squeaking so much, I realized. It's never been used.

"My, what is he so excited about?" Miss Gaunt stared at Homer.

"Usually he sleeps all day," Marcy told her.

Miss Gaunt moved a few steps closer. She peered into Homer's cage. Homer ran even harder.

Miss Gaunt rapped playfully on the top of the cage.

"Good little hamster," she said softly. "You'll be quiet now, won't you?"

The squeaking sound stopped immediately. Homer jumped off the wheel and plopped down in the sawdust at the bottom of his cage.

Whoa, I thought. Miss Gaunt should open a hamster obedience school. Homer never does anything *I* tell him to.

"What do you children do after attendance?"

Chris's hand flew up. I knew what he was up to. But this time I planned to beat him to it.

I shot my hand up, too.

"Yes, Zachariah?"

"Right after attendance we have recess, Miss Gaunt," I announced. "And right after recess we go to lunch."

Most of the kids laughed. It will be a while before Chris calls me a dweeb again, I thought!

"Oh, I just love a boy with a sense of humor," Miss Gaunt said. "Tell me, Zachariah. Are you so amusing when you stay after school and write 'I Promise Never to Be a Smart Aleck' a hundred times on the blackboard?"

Miss Gaunt snatched up the pointer in the chalk tray. She walked toward my desk. When Chris played tricks on the substitutes, they never punished him. How come it backfired when I tried it?

"Zachariah, you didn't really mean to be so rude, did you?" Miss Gaunt asked. With each word she rapped the pointer on the top of my desk.

"No, Miss Gaunt," I mumbled, watching the pointer.

"I knew that," Miss Gaunt replied. "The moment I saw you, I just knew you were not that kind of boy."

"It's just that I—"

"Oh, you don't need to apologize. Not to me," she said. "You and I are going to get along fine."

Then she placed her fingers under my chin. Forcing me to stare up at her.

"I'll be keeping my eye on you, Zachariah Pepper!"

Even through her gloves, her touch was cold.
Ice cold.

4

"**O**h, Zach-a-ri-ah!" I heard Chris yell.

I spotted him and Marcy on the other side of the cafeteria. I wove around the long tables, then plopped down on the bench across from them. Chris leaned forward and made loud kissing noises. "Zach-a-ri-ah, such a bea-u-ti-ful name!" he cried in that clear voice Miss Gaunt liked so much.

"So what do you think of Miss Gaunt?" I asked, trying to ignore him.

"I think she needs to be arrested by the fashion police," Tiffany Loomis called from the corner of the table. "Where did she find those clothes?"

18

"Maybe she thought today was Halloween," Danny Abernathy volunteered.

"Yeah," Tiffany agreed. "But her clothes are even spookier than a Halloween costume."

"Did you notice how pale she is?" I asked. "I wonder if she ever goes out in the sun."

Marcy finished her sandwich. She stared off into space for a moment. Then she said, "Miss Gaunt is kind of strange, but she's really good at teaching things. Like that spelling trick about the word *weird:* '*Weird* is weird—it doesn't follow the *i* before *e* except after *c* rule.'"

"She is a pretty good teacher," I said. "But that's probably because she's been teaching forever. She must be a hundred years old."

"You know what I think about Miss Gaunt?" Chris asked. "I think she's in love with Zach-a-riah."

"Cut it out," I snapped back.

"She did pick you to feed Homer this week," Tiffany said, laughing.

I glanced up at the cafeteria clock. Ten minutes till lunch period ended. "I think I'll feed him now. I want to give him part of my apple."

"I'll come, too," Marcy said. "I have a piece of celery left.

19

"I'll help," Chris added. "But he's not getting any of my lunch."

The three of us grabbed our stuff and headed back to our classroom.

"Hello, children," Miss Gaunt called as we trooped in. "What eager students you are. Class doesn't begin for another ten minutes."

"We wanted to feed Homer his lunch," I explained.

"Very conscientious of you, Zachariah," she said.

"Thanks," I muttered. I waited for Chris to start laughing. He didn't. He was staring over my shoulder.

"Look!" he said, pointing. "Something terrible has happened to Homer!"

"Did the ghost dog get him?" I shot back. I couldn't believe Chris thought I'd fall for another one of his stupid jokes so soon.

"I'm not kidding!" Chris declared. "Something weird is going on!"

Marcy peered into Homer's cage. "Chris is right!"

I turned around and stared at the hamster.

Every single hair on Homer's body had turned white.

5

All the kids returned from lunch. We huddled around Homer's cage.

"Maybe someone switched hamsters on us," Chris said. "Maybe it *isn't* Homer."

"Oh, it's Homer, all right," Marcy insisted. "Look at his ear. See the little rip in it? Remember when he had the accident? It's still Homer."

"I've heard of this happening to people if something really scary happens to them," I said. "I didn't know it could happen to animals, too."

But it did happen. And I knew who was to blame.

21

Miss Gaunt.

I remembered how strange Homer acted this morning when she stood near his cage. She must have something to do with this, I thought. She must.

"What's going on here?" Miss Gaunt asked, coming up behind us.

"Homer turned white," Chris explained, stepping back from the cage so Miss Gaunt could see.

The minute Homer spotted Miss Gaunt, his entire body began to shake. And he burrowed his head under some sawdust.

He's trembling, I noticed. Animals are supposed to be good judges of people. And Homer is terrified. Anyone can see that.

Uh-oh, I thought. What if Miss Gaunt really is—a ghost!

"Turning white is not that unusual," Miss Gaunt said, interrupting my thoughts. "Many animals turn white as winter comes. It's their camouflage."

"You mean it protects them from being eaten by other animals?" Danny asked.

Miss Gaunt smiled at him. "Very good, Danny," she said. "It is much more difficult to see a white animal against white snow. And more

22

difficult to see means more difficult to catch—and eat."

"Does anyone know of another animal that changes color in the winter?"

"An ermine?" Marcy called out.

"Well done, Marcy," Miss Gaunt said. "Or it is possible that Homer has a vitamin deficiency. That can often make an animal's fur change color. Perhaps we can ask your science teacher."

When I thought about it, Miss Gaunt's explanations made sense. "Oh, boy. I almost did it again," I muttered. "I almost freaked out over nothing. I have to finish *Power Kids!* tonight."

Miss Gaunt clapped her hands. "Finish feeding Homer, children. We have work to do."

I pulled out the hamster's water bottle and filled it in the sink in the back of the room. Miss Gaunt followed me.

"You seemed very interested in my little science lesson, Zachariah."

I didn't know what to say. I spied Chris staring at us. His mouth curled up in his stupid grin.

Miss Gaunt didn't wait for an answer. "I enjoy teaching so much more when I have an enthusiastic student," she told me.

I nodded quickly and hurried back to Homer's

cage with the bottle. On the way I passed Chris's seat. "Here comes the teacher's pet," he whispered to Tiffany. She giggled.

By the time I returned to my desk, Miss Gaunt had started the history lesson. "This afternoon we will continue your study of the American Revolution," she announced. She opened a box and dumped a bunch of old metal soldiers on her desk.

"Danny, I would like you to lead the British," she instructed. "Come collect your soldiers."

As Danny headed toward the front of the room, Miss Gaunt asked, "Who would like to take the role of George Washington?" Lots of kids raised their hands. Her eyes searched the room.

I stared down at my desk. The soldiers looked like fun, but I didn't want to get chosen for anything. Not by her.

"Zachariah, would you lead the rebel forces?" she called.

I heard Chris snicker.

I shuffled up to Miss Gaunt's desk and gathered up a handful of soldiers.

That's when I noticed something on the side of Miss Gaunt's neck. A deep purple blotch. Kind of long and bumpy.

I didn't want Miss Gaunt to notice me staring. I

24

glanced down at my soldiers. Then I stole another quick peek.

The thing on Miss Gaunt's neck moved.

It was alive!

Miss Gaunt had a fat, slimy worm crawling on her neck!

6

The worm was thick and wet looking. I watched as Miss Gaunt reached up and picked it off her neck. Then she squooshed it between her gloved fingers and tossed it into the wastebasket.

I glanced at the other kids. They were all gathered around a huge map Miss Gaunt had spread on the floor. No one had noticed a thing.

Maybe it was a piece of fuzz, I tried to convince myself. But I didn't think so.

I didn't talk to anybody the rest of the afternoon. After history we made a card for Miss Prescott. Then it was time to go home.

Marcy, Chris, and I left school together. But I

didn't say anything to them about what I had seen.

That night I made sure I finished reading *Power Kids!*

Okay, Zack, I told myself as I opened the classroom door the next morning, it's power time. You did *not* see a worm on Miss Gaunt's neck yesterday. Remember what *Power Kids!* said: You see what you expect to see.

And you always expect to see something scary, I reminded myself.

But not anymore!

I calmly walked over to my desk and sat down. I studied Miss Gaunt's neck carefully. Pasty white skin. Nothing else. No worm.

Miss Gaunt took the attendance and I began to relax. We said the Pledge of Allegiance.

Then we began a math lesson. "Who would like to go to the blackboard and show the class how to multiply decimals?" Miss Gaunt asked.

I tried to make myself invisible. I scrunched down in my chair. I was safe. Lots of kids waved their hands.

"How about you showing us, Zachariah?" Miss Gaunt suggested.

"Actually, I'm not all that good at decimals, Miss Gaunt," I admitted.

"That's why we come to school, isn't it?" Miss Gaunt asked. "So we can learn to do better?"

"But you see, I'm not—" I began, but my mouth grew dry. My voice cracked.

"Not feeling well, dear?" Miss Gaunt asked in her high little voice. "You're not coming down with a sore throat, are you?" She walked down the aisle toward me. "Do you need to see the school nurse?"

She reached out to press her hand on my forehead.

"Honest, Miss Gaunt," I said, pulling away. "I'm fine." I didn't want to feel the touch of her icy fingers again.

Miss Gaunt stretched out her hand once more. Her white glove smelled a little like dirt. And it looked grimy.

As she placed her hand on my forehead, I remembered how cold my grandmother's hands were sometimes. Grandma said it was because of poor circulation—it happens when people get older.

I forced myself to sit still. Miss Gaunt couldn't help that her hands were cold.

But when she touched me, I felt the cold all the way inside my head. A sharp stinging pain.

"Well, you don't have a fever, Zachariah," Miss

Gaunt said. "Could it be that you're afraid of making a mistake—and the other children teasing you?"

I shrugged. "I don't understand decimals at all."

"Well, no one's going to laugh at you, Zachariah. Not in my classroom. Besides, I never met a Zachariah who didn't multiply decimals beautifully!"

I glanced around the room. None of the kids seemed as if they were about to laugh. Not even Chris. But even if they didn't laugh now, I knew they'd make fun of me after school.

But I had no choice. I approached the chalkboard.

"Thirty-seven point twenty-nine multiplied by four hundred and seventy-two point sixty-three," Miss Gaunt instructed. "Write it on the blackboard, Zachariah."

My hand trembled. I could barely write out the numbers.

"Go ahead," she said. "Now write down the answer."

I swallowed hard. "I can't," I said quietly.

"Why is that, Zachariah?" Miss Gaunt asked.

"Because I don't know how." Is Miss Gaunt going to make me stand up here all day? I was beginning to panic. I felt my ears turn hot.

"You can do it, Zachariah," Miss Gaunt said firmly. "I know you can, dear."

She stepped toward me.

Squeak. Squeak. Squeak. I heard Homer in his cage. Running wildly on his treadmill again.

"Be still, Homer," Miss Gaunt called. "Let Zachariah concentrate now."

The squeaking stopped abruptly.

My hand floated into the air. I squeezed the chalk between my fingers, but I didn't feel anything. My fingers were numb.

What's happening? It felt as though a big magnet was tugging my hand up. Up to the chalkboard.

Then I began to write. My hand wrote number after number.

"Very good, Zachariah," Miss Gaunt said proudly. "I knew you could do it."

But I knew I didn't do it. Something else did. Something else had control of my arm!

7

My arm flopped back to my side. The chalk flew from my fingers. It broke against the floor.

"Well done, Zachariah," Miss Gaunt said. "You may return to your seat."

I stumbled down the aisle to my desk and slid into the chair. My arm felt itchy. Prickly.

I stared down at my hand and wiggled my fingers.

I raised my eyes to Miss Gaunt. She smiled at me proudly—and winked.

She did it, I thought. Miss Gaunt forced me to write the correct answer. She moved my hand!

Power Kids! didn't cover anything like this. I

had to tell Marcy and Chris. This wasn't my imagination. This was for real.

When the lunch bell finally rang, I bolted out the door. I waited a few feet down the hall for Marcy and Chris.

"You did great in math," Marcy called when she spotted me.

"Yeah," Chris agreed.

"It wasn't me," I told them.

"What do you mean?" Chris asked.

I motioned for them to move away from the door. I didn't want Miss Gaunt—or anyone else—to hear what I had to say.

"It wasn't me," I repeated. "I didn't know the answers, and I didn't move my hand."

"What?" Chris demanded.

"Miss Gaunt took control of me. She made my hand move," I whispered. "She's a ghost. I know it."

Chris clutched his chest and staggered back a few steps. "No!" he cried. Then he started to laugh.

"Come on, Zack," Marcy pleaded.

"Think about it," I insisted. "Homer turned white on the day she started. Your hair turns white when you get scared, right?"

"My mother said her hair turned white the day she had me," Chris joked.

Marcy ignored him. "Miss Gaunt explained about Homer turning white, remember? Camouflage or vitamin deficiency."

"But other strange things have happened, too," I insisted.

"Yeah," Chris chimed in. "Don't forget—Zack got the right answer to a decimal question!"

Marcy slapped Chris on the shoulder.

"He's right, Marcy. I didn't know the answer. I'm telling you—she moved my hand! And there's something else," I said. "I saw a worm on Miss Gaunt's neck yesterday, and it didn't even bother her. She just squooshed it."

"Gross!" Marcy exclaimed.

"Cool," Chris added.

"So what are we going to do about Miss Gaunt?" I asked.

"Bring her some Worms-Away?" Chris suggested. "That's what we give my cousin's dog."

I didn't really expect any help from Chris. But what would Marcy say?

Marcy shook her head. "She *is* really creepy, Zack. But she's not a ghost. There's no such thing as ghosts."

Not even Marcy—my best friend—believed me. What was I going to do?

Marcy grabbed my arm and pulled me down the hall. "Let's go eat. Maybe you'll feel better after lunch."

"I'm so hungry I could eat a ghost horse," Chris said as he followed us to the cafeteria.

I stopped suddenly.

"What's wrong?" Marcy asked.

"Nothing. I left my lunch in my desk. I'll meet you guys inside."

I dashed down the hall. If Miss Gaunt is still in the classroom, I'll skip lunch, I thought. Because I'm definitely not going in there alone.

I peeked inside. The room was empty.

I hurried to my desk and opened the top.

Something white fluttered to the ground.

It was one of Miss Gaunt's gloves!

8

Why was Miss Gaunt's glove in my desk? I wondered. She must have been snooping around, I guessed. And dropped it there by accident.

I didn't say anything about the glove to Marcy or Chris during lunch. In fact, I didn't say much of anything. I didn't really feel like talking.

After lunch we piled into the classroom. Chris's hand shot up before Miss Gaunt could say a word.

Oh, no. I stiffened in my seat. He's going to tell everyone what I said. He's going to tell them Miss Gaunt is a ghost.

"Miss Gaunt," Chris began. "Halloween is coming up—"

I sank down. And let out a long sigh.

"And Miss Prescott said we could have a party on Friday," Chris announced.

"Then we shall have one," Miss Gaunt told him. "Thank you for bringing it up, Chris."

Miss Gaunt turned to the chalkboard. "Let's begin with a list of what we need."

"Cookies," Debbie called out.

Miss Gaunt started to write on the board. The chalk snapped and fell from her fingers. Bobby Dreyfuss picked it up for her. He sat in the front row.

I could hardly read the words she wrote. The letters were all different sizes. And very wobbly.

"Decorations," Marcy suggested.

The chalk screeched across the board as Miss Gaunt continued the list. She dropped the chalk again.

"Is something wrong with your hand?" Bobby asked as he picked up the chalk again and handed it to Miss Gaunt.

"It's just a little arthritis," Miss Gaunt said. "It happens when we get older."

"Do you have arthritis in your other hand, too, Miss Gaunt?" Bobby asked.

I noticed that Miss Gaunt held her right hand tucked inside her blouse. Doesn't she usually write with that hand? I thought she did, but I couldn't remember.

"Why don't we keep our attention on what we need for the party," Miss Gaunt suggested.

"But I only—" Bobby started.

"Please, Bobby," Miss Gaunt said stiffly. "Let's go on with the list."

Miss Gaunt dropped the chalk in the tray. "Perhaps we don't need a list. Debbie, would you like to volunteer for the liquid refreshment?" she asked.

"You mean drinks?" Debbie asked uncertainly.

"Exactly, dear," Miss Gaunt replied. "People enjoy cider at Halloween parties. Do you think you could manage that?"

"Yes, Miss Gaunt," Debbie said.

"How about cups and plates?"

Danny waved his hand in the air. "My dad works over at Dalby's," he told her. "He can get them for us free, I bet."

"Why, how nice," Miss Gaunt said. "Will you thank your father for us?"

"Can we play games?" Chris asked. "We've been collecting money to buy some."

"What kinds of games did you have in mind, Chris?" Miss Gaunt asked. "Something like Pin the Tail on the Donkey?"

"More like Pin the Fangs on the Werewolf," Chris said. "Or how about Dead Man's Bluff?"

"That sounds a bit frightening, doesn't it?" Miss Gaunt asked. "Do you children really enjoy these games?"

"It's Halloween," Chris insisted. "It's supposed to be scary. I bet we could find some cool games down at Dalby's."

"Why don't you try Shop Till You Drop," Miss Gaunt said. "It's a new place over by the Stop 'N' Shop. Take Zack and Marcy with you. They can help pick out decorations there. But nothing too horrifying, please."

The last bell rang. I leaped out of my chair and headed for the door.

"Would you stay behind, Zachariah?" Miss Gaunt called.

"Just me?" I asked.

"Don't worry," she said. "I only want to ask you a little question, dear."

Miss Gaunt waited until everyone left the classroom. Then she closed the door and turned toward me.

"May I have it?" she asked.

"Have *what,* Miss Gaunt?"

"You have something that belongs to me, Zachariah," she stated.

"I didn't take anything," I said. "Honest."

"But I saw you put it in your pocket, dear," she said. "It should still be there."

I stuck my hand into my pocket. Her glove. I forgot that I shoved it in there.

I pulled the glove out. It slipped from my fingers and fluttered to the floor.

"Do you think you could pick that up for me, Zachariah?" Miss Gaunt asked.

As I bent over I said, "I'm sorry about your arthritis, Miss Gaunt." Then I held the glove out to her.

"What arthritis, dear?"

"But you told Bobby—"

"Oh, Bobby is so nosy," Miss Gaunt declared. "I had to tell him something, didn't I?"

She reached for the glove with her left hand. Then she whipped her right hand out from the fold of her blouse.

And there wasn't any skin on her fingers!

Only bones.

The bones of a skeleton.

9

"**H**er hand—it was horrible," I told Chris and Marcy. "It didn't have any skin on it."

My knees began to buckle as I described it.

We were on our way to the party decoration store—the one Miss Gaunt told us about.

"And we shouldn't go to this store," I added. "We shouldn't do anything Miss Gaunt tells us to do."

"Get a grip," Chris said.

"How long did you see her hand for, anyway?"

"Just for a second," I admitted. "Until she put her glove back on. But that was long enough. I'm telling you—Miss Gaunt is a ghost."

40

"Come on, Zack. That's what happens when people grow old," Marcy explained. "They get very thin."

"It wasn't just thin," I insisted. "It was bony— like a real skeleton's hand!"

"Look! There it is," Chris said, pointing. "The party store."

I gazed across the street. There it was, all right. Miss Gaunt said its name was Shop Till You Drop. But the sign out front read Shop Till You Drop *Dead.*

"Oooooo. There could be ghosts inside, Zack!" Chris joked when he noticed the sign. "Are you sure you want to go in?"

"Don't be an idiot, Chris," Marcy replied, crossing the street.

"I don't think it's open," I said as we neared the store. "I don't see any lights on."

Marcy was the first to reach the front door. "Oh, I get it," she said. "Someone's painted the windows black." She pressed her face against the glass. She cupped her hands around her eyes. "I can't see anything in there."

She pushed on the door. It opened silently.

Inside a single dirty bulb hung from the ceiling. It swung back and forth, back and forth—casting creepy shadows on the walls.

The store appeared to be huge—but it was hard to tell in the dim light. It also appeared to be empty.

"Hello! Is anybody here?" Chris yelled. No one answered.

The door banged shut behind us.

"Anybody here?" Chris called again.

I heard a soft rustling sound. Then silence.

My eyes adjusted to the darkness. The store was lined with tall wooden shelves that stretched almost to the ceiling. Beyond them, the back of the store was bathed in a deep purple glow.

"Let's go to Dalby's," Marcy said. "This place *is* creepy."

"Yeah," I agreed.

"I want to stay," Chris argued. "I bet we can find some cool Halloween stuff here. Besides, I promised my mom I'd be home by four. I don't have time to go to another place."

Chris hurried down one of the narrow aisles.

I followed him. I didn't want him telling everyone in school that I freaked out in a Halloween store.

Everything smelled strange. Kind of moldy—like old mushrooms. And the floor felt bumpy and uneven. I heard something crunch under my feet.

"How are we supposed to find anything when

42

we can't *see* anything?" Marcy muttered behind me.

We took a few more steps.

Crunch, crunch, crunch.

"What is making that noise?" Marcy asked.

I stared down at the floor. "I can't tell," I answered. "It sounds like we're walking on peanut shells or something."

I crouched down, peered at my shoes—and saw them. Millions of them.

Millions of slimy black beetles swarming all over the floor.

Marcy spotted them, too. We both gasped.

Suddenly a bright overhead light flashed on. Marcy kneeled to study the beetles. Then she picked one up!

"Plastic," she announced. "Plastic bugs."

"Uh, I guess they decorated the whole store for Halloween," I said. "Pretty cool, huh?"

We both laughed.

"Hey, Marcy, the light that went on—who threw the switch?" I asked. We both glanced around. No one was in sight.

"Where's Chris?" Marcy asked.

"He was right in front of me a minute ago," I told her.

I figured Chris was probably hiding down one of

43

the aisles. Waiting to jump out at us. Well, he's not going to get me this time, I told myself. I scanned the shelves, searching for something creepy to use to scare him first.

The shelves were crammed with all kinds of strange stuff. A jar full of glass eyeballs. A withered hand. A mesh bag filled with small bones. And some cool masks.

I grabbed two masks. I pulled a gorilla mask over my head. It smelled rotten inside—like spoiled meat. But I didn't care.

I handed the other mask to Marcy. It was really gross. A monster face with one eyeball hanging from a bloody thread.

"Chris!" I shouted as loud as I could. "Where are you?"

Then I leaned in close to Marcy and whispered, "I bet Chris is hiding around that corner. Let's scare him before he can scare us."

Marcy smiled and slipped the mask over her head.

We tiptoed to the end of the aisle. I hope Chris doesn't hear those stupid plastic bugs crunching, I thought.

I turned to Marcy and held up three fingers. She nodded. We'd both jump around the corner on the count of three.

44

I gave the signal and leaped out. I beat on my chest and howled.

Marcy screeched—high and long. I was impressed. She really sounded scary.

Someone *was* standing around that corner, but it wasn't Chris. It was a man. The strangest man I had ever seen. His head was big and round—the size of a basketball. The pasty skin on his face stretched right up over his bald scalp. He wore a shiny black cape that trailed to the floor.

Marcy dug her fingernails into my arm and pointed—to something lying on the ground at the man's feet.

It was Chris. Lying absolutely still.

A trickle of blood ran from the corner of his mouth.

10

"**W**hat did you do to Chris!" I screamed. Marcy and I ripped off our masks and fell to Chris's side.

"Chris!" Marcy cried. "Chris, are you okay?"

Chris's eyes fluttered. He struggled to sit up. Then he cried, "Gotcha!"

Marcy and I glared at him.

"Come on, guys. Say something," Chris whined. "Hey, don't you think this fake blood is great?"

"Yes, it is delicious, isn't it?" the bald man replied.

Chris jerked his head back. "Who are you?" he asked, scrambling to his feet.

"I?" the man asked. "Why, I am Mr. Sangfwad.

46

The owner of this establishment. How may I serve you?" He stroked the head of a small, furry animal buried in his arms.

"We're here for Halloween," Chris mumbled.

"To buy games and decorations for our class party," Marcy added.

"Oh, oh, oh!" Mr. Sangfwad exclaimed. "Evangeline must have sent you!" Then he grinned, showing off a big dark hole where his two front teeth used to be.

"Evangeline?" Chris asked.

"From Shadyside Middle School," Mr. Sangfwad explained. "The substitute teacher."

"Oh!" I groaned. "You must mean Miss Gaunt."

"Yes. Yes. Miss Gaunt. And you must be Zachariah," Mr. Sangfwad said, studying me carefully. "Evangeline speaks very highly of you."

"Do you really know Miss Gaunt?" I asked.

"Why, of course I do. Miss Gaunt and I have been friends in Shadyside forever. Haven't we, Phoebe?" he crooned to the little gray pet in his arms.

"But I've lived here my whole life," I said. "I've never seen either of you before."

"Life is strange, isn't it?" Mr. Sangfwad replied.

47

That wasn't exactly the answer I was looking for.

With both hands Mr. Sangfwad lifted his pet high in the air.

Its tiny black eyes popped into view.

Then its whiskers.

Then its sharp yellow teeth.

A rat!

"You're holding a rat!" I cried.

"Oh, don't let Phoebe scare you." Mr. Sangfwad kissed the top of the rat's head. "She's quite sweet."

"She could bite you!" Chris warned.

"Rats will be rats," Mr. Sangfwad said.

"You could die!" Marcy exclaimed.

"I said she was sweet," Mr. Sangfwad replied. "I didn't say she was harmless!"

Mr. Sangfwad placed Phoebe on the floor. I hoped she would scurry away. But instead she circled our feet.

"Now. Exactly what kind of games would you like for your Halloween party?" Mr. Sangfwad asked.

"Do you have Pin the Fangs on the Werewolf and Dead Man's Bluff?" Chris asked.

"Why, of course," Mr. Sangfwad answered. "They are in aisle three, and—" Chris headed

48

over to the aisle before Mr. Sangfwad finished. "Don't forget Spin the Zombie and Power Ghouls," he called after him.

"Do you have Halloween decorations?" Marcy asked politely.

"Halloween decorations? For Evangeline's students? Of course I do. I suppose you want black and orange streamers—that sort of thing."

"Exactly," I told him. I couldn't wait to leave the store. Mr. Sangfwad gave me the creeps.

When we had everything we needed, Marcy and I met Chris at the cash register.

Mr. Sangfwad rang up the order. Marcy paid him with the money we had collected in school.

"I'm afraid I've run out of bags," Mr. Sangfwad announced, searching under the counter. "I have some in back if you would wait just a moment."

Chris checked his watch. "It's ten to four. I've gotta go. My mom will kill me if I'm not home on time today."

"Go ahead," Marcy told him. "Zack and I can handle this stuff."

"Great." Chris hurried out the front door. "See ya!"

Marcy and I waited by the cash register. I shifted from one foot to the other. I wanted to get out of there.

"What's taking him so long?" I complained.

"He just left," Marcy said. "Be patient."

I kept checking my watch. "Maybe we can carry this stuff without bags," I suggested. "We've already paid. Let's go."

"Shhh," Marcy whispered. "Here he comes."

"Okeydokey," Mr. Sangfwad sang out cheerfully, approaching the counter. He piled all our decorations into a bag.

"Now, are you sure you have everything you need for your party?" he asked. "Halloween is very, very important to Evangeline."

Then he stared directly into my eyes and added, "I know *you* wouldn't want to disappoint her."

11

"**W**ell?" I demanded once we stepped outside. "Do you believe me now?"

"Do I believe what?" Marcy asked.

"That Miss Gaunt is a ghost," I shot back.

"Zack, you're being ridiculous."

"How can you say that?" I practically shrieked. "Everything about her is totally weird—including her creepy friend Mr. Sangfwad and his horrible store."

"Mr. Sangfwad was kind of strange. . . ." Marcy's voice trailed off.

"*Kind* of strange?" I screeched. "He had a rat for a pet! And didn't you hear what he said—that he and Miss Gaunt have lived in Shadyside *forever?*"

"So, what's your point?" Marcy asked.

"Don't you think it's kind of funny that we've never seen either of them before?"

"Well . . ." Marcy began.

"Come with me after school tomorrow," I interrupted. "I'm going to follow Miss Gaunt. And I'm going to get real proof."

"Fine," Marcy said.

"Then—you mean—you believe me?" I asked excitedly.

"No," Marcy replied. "I'm going with you to prove once and for all that there are no such things as ghosts!"

"She *is* a ghost, Marcy. You'll see!"

Was I right? Was Miss Gaunt really a ghost?

I wasn't sure of anything anymore.

But we were going to follow her. And we were finally going to find out.

I had no idea what my decision would lead to.

12

The next morning we rode our bikes to school. We'd use them afterward to follow Miss Gaunt.

I couldn't wait for the final bell to ring. But by the end of the day, I began to feel scared. What if Miss Gaunt caught us following her?

Even if she wasn't a ghost, she'd be pretty angry. And we'd be in tons of trouble.

If she was a ghost, things could be a lot worse.

What did ghosts do to people who stumbled in their way?

I didn't know. And I didn't want to find out.

After the last bell rang, Marcy and I hid alongside the school trophy case in the front hall. We watched all the kids leave.

Then Miss Gaunt appeared. She approached the school's two heavy steel front doors. I noticed how tiny and frail she seemed in front of them. I wondered if she would have trouble opening them. I always do. But when she grabbed the exit bar and pushed, the door flew open.

"Did you see that?" I whispered to Marcy. "Did you see how easily she opened the door? Now what do you think?"

Marcy stared at me—as if I were nuts.

No sense in starting an argument with her, I decided. We would both find out the truth soon enough.

When the door swung closed, we crept over to it. We opened it a crack and watched Miss Gaunt climb down the steps.

She headed across the school yard. Then she ducked behind some bushes. We dashed outside.

"Oh, no!" I cried. "We've lost her already!"

"No, we haven't," Marcy said, jabbing me in the ribs.

She was right. There was Miss Gaunt—out from behind the bushes. Pedaling a bike!

"I can't believe Miss Gaunt rides a bike," I said as we ran over to ours. "She's too old for that."

We leaped on our bikes and charged after her.

By the time we reached the first intersection, Miss Gaunt had disappeared.

"Do you think she turned left or right on Park Drive?" Marcy asked.

"I don't know. We'll just have to guess."

The light turned green, and we turned right on Park. There was Miss Gaunt—directly ahead of us. "Yes!" I cried.

Miss Gaunt turned right again. Onto Fear Street.

I remembered what my brother, Kevin, told me about Fear Street—that the most evil ghosts of all haunted it.

"It figures," I moaned to Marcy. "Miss Gaunt lives on Fear Street."

"Even if she does live on Fear Street, that doesn't mean she's a ghost," Marcy said firmly.

We rode by the houses on Fear Street. Some of them were all fixed up. A lot of them were wrecks, with sagging porches and peeling paint.

And some were totally abandoned. Looming above all of them was the burned-out shell of the Fear mansion. That one was definitely the scariest.

We pedaled quickly by the mansion. Following Miss Gaunt around one curve after another.

The afternoon sun was beginning to set. Fear Street was really spooky in the dark. And we didn't see a single car going in either direction. No joggers. No other bikes. No people out for a stroll.

My head began to throb. It was too scary here. I wanted to turn around and go home.

I was about to suggest it, but Marcy spoke first. "Look! She's slowing down."

"I bet we're coming to her house!" I exclaimed.

I watched Miss Gaunt slip off her bike.

She leaned it against two huge iron gates.

The gates of the Fear Street Cemetery!

13

I slowly reached out and pushed open the iron gate. It felt as cold as Miss Gaunt's fingers.

I glanced over at Marcy. I could tell she was waiting for me to go in first. "So what do you think now?" I asked her.

"People visit graveyards, you know," Marcy replied. But I thought I heard a little quiver in her voice.

I slipped through the gate, Marcy right behind me. I felt like an intruder. The stone angels seemed to stare down at me disapprovingly.

We ran from grave to grave. Ducking behind each tombstone before we sprinted to the next. We had to be very careful. We definitely did not want Miss Gaunt to spot us.

A sudden gust of wind set the autumn leaves swirling. Swirling around the tombstones.

The last rays of the sun had faded. And I shivered in the blast of chilly air.

Miss Gaunt glided between the graves. Marcy and I followed.

"Zack," Marcy whispered, pointing to the ground. "Look!"

I glanced down. A whirling gray mist covered our feet. "Hey! Where did that come from?"

The mist slowly rose to our knees. We watched as it grew thicker. And higher.

"Maybe we should head back," I said anxiously. Then I changed my mind. "No, we can't. We've got to follow Miss Gaunt!"

But when I gazed up, Miss Gaunt had disappeared!

"Where did she go?" I cried.

"I don't know," Marcy replied, squinting to see through the churning gray spray. "The mist is too thick. I think we should go back."

"Okay. Okay," I agreed. "But which way is back?"

"Just follow me," Marcy replied. Then she broke into a run, dashing between the gravestones.

"Slow down, Marcy!" I cried out, trying to keep up.

Marcy tripped over something—probably a rock. I couldn't tell. The mist covered everything now. She hit the ground with a soft thud. But in a second she was up again, running faster.

"Marcy!" I cried out. "Slow down. I'm going to lose you."

Marcy stumbled once more.

I spotted her arms waving frantically through the mist.

"Zack!" she screamed. "Help me!"

Then she sank totally out of sight.

I waited. Waited for her to jump up—so I would know which way to go.

But Marcy didn't appear.

"Marcy!" I yelled. "Where are you?"

Marcy had vanished.

14

"**M**arcy!" I called out, louder this time. "Marcy!"

No answer.

I inched forward.

The mist swirled all around me now. It was impossible to see.

Where was Marcy? Had she run into Miss Gaunt? Did Miss Gaunt have her trapped right now?

My heart hammered away in my chest. The mist had grown icy, and I began to shiver. But I pressed on, calling Marcy's name out every few steps.

"Marcy! Where are you? Marcy!"

"Over here, Zack!"

Marcy!

I stepped in the direction of her voice—and my legs flew out from under me.

I plunged down—down into total darkness.

And then, finally, I landed—somewhere damp and very, very dark.

"Oooh," I groaned, rubbing my head.

As I fumbled to sit up, a cold hand groped in the darkness and grabbed my arm.

"Let me go!" I screamed, trying desperately to shake loose.

"Zack! Stop it! It's me."

"Marcy!" I cried with relief. "Where are we?"

"I think we've fallen into a grave."

"A grave? Oh, gross!" I shouted. "Are we—are we alone down here?"

"Of course we're alone down here," Marcy snapped. "That's why we fell. We fell into an empty grave."

"Okay. Okay," I said. "I just thought that . . . maybe . . . Miss Gaunt was down here, too."

"Zack, she was headed in the other direction when we lost her."

"Oh. Right," I said.

Marcy sighed.

"It's really disgusting down here," I said, glancing around the underground pit. "How are we going to get out?"

"Good question," Marcy replied.

I stood up. Then Marcy and I tried to fling ourselves out of the grave.

But the walls were too high.

We searched the sides of the grave for a rock, a tree root, something to grab on to—to hoist ourselves up. But the dirt simply slipped through our fingers.

"Hey, I have an idea," I said to Marcy. "Give me a boost. Once I'm out, I can help pull you up."

Marcy knit her hands together. I slipped my foot into them and pushed off with all my might. My hands flew up and found the grave opening.

"I'm out!" I shouted.

I hung from the grave's edge, my feet dangling below. Marcy shoved my legs up as I pulled myself to the ground above.

Then I leaned over and dragged Marcy up.

Marcy tumbled out, and we both toppled backward onto the ground.

"Oh, no," Marcy moaned.

"Are you hurt?" I asked.

Marcy didn't answer my question. She simply

stared ahead. And even in the dark I could see she was trembling. Finally she said,

"Read it, Zack."

Marcy was staring at a gravestone. The gravestone at the head of the empty grave.

It was very old.

I could barely make out the engraving.

I moved up close to it, squinted, and read:

EVANGELINE GAUNT
BORN 1769   DIED 1845
REST IN PEACE

"It's *her* grave!" I screamed. "We were in *her* grave!"

15

"She *is* a ghost!" I cried. "Let's get out of here. Before she finds us!"

We charged through the cemetery, stumbling over rocks and dodging graves.

We ran and ran. But we were nowhere near the entrance.

"It's a maze!" Marcy cried. "We're going around in circles."

I stopped. My eyes darted left and right. Trying to find a clue to guide us.

The mist began to lift, and I spotted some hedges a few feet away. "Let's go through there!" I cried.

I parted the hedges and held them back so Marcy could squeeze through. The little thorns ripped into my hands. But I didn't care.

As I shoved through the hedge after Marcy, I yelled, "Look! The entrance! We're almost there!"

We dashed to the gates, jumped on our bikes, and pedaled as hard as we could. We didn't speak until we reached Marcy's house.

"*Now* do you believe me?"

Marcy nodded, gasping for breath. "Miss Gaunt is a ghost. What are we going to do?"

I wiped the sweat from my forehead. "We have to tell the rest of the kids as soon as we reach school tomorrow," I said. "Meet me outside the main entrance at eight-fifteen. We'll catch them before they go in—and warn them. . . ."

I paced back and forth the next morning in front of the school. I glanced at my watch for the hundreth time—8:25 . . . 8:27 . . . 8:31 . . .

Not it was 8:45 and still no Marcy.

Where could she be? I wondered. Most of the kids had arrived and gone inside.

I didn't stop them.

I didn't want to tell them about Miss Gaunt alone. I told Marcy we would do it together.

Besides, I knew no one would believe *me*. I needed Marcy there.

I glanced at my watch one last time—9:00.

I had to go in.

But now I was worried—really worried about Marcy.

Where was she?

Did Miss Gaunt see us yesterday?

Did she know we were following her?

Did she find Marcy this morning and do something horrible to her?

I bolted through the classroom door just as Miss Gaunt began taking attendance. I shot a glance at Marcy's seat. It was empty.

"Abernathy, Danny."

"Here, Miss Gaunt."

I studied Miss Gaunt as she called roll. Her high little voice sounded the same as always. She didn't seem upset—or angry.

"Hassler, Chris."

"Here, Miss Gaunt."

I wondered if Miss Gaunt could tell how upset *I* was.

I held my breath until Miss Gaunt reached Marcy's name.

"Novi, Marcy."

No answer.

66

"Can anyone tell me why Marcy Novi is not here this morning?" she asked.

No one volunteered.

"Oh, I just remembered," Miss Gaunt said. "Marcy's out for a few days, I'm afraid."

"Is she sick, Miss Gaunt?" Tiffany asked. "Should we send her a card?"

"I doubt it would reach her in time," Miss Gaunt said.

"In time for what?" Tiffany asked.

In time for what?

Suddenly my hands began to shake.

"Really, Tiffany," Miss Gaunt replied. "Would you like to hear someone telling the whole class your family secrets?"

"It's a *secret?*" Tiffany asked excitedly.

Miss Gaunt shook her head in disapproval. Then she continued on.

"Reynolds," she called out sharply.

"Here, Miss Gaunt!"

"Steinford."

"Here, Miss Gaunt!"

Marcy was in trouble. I have to find her, I thought. And fast!

I didn't hear a word Miss Gaunt said all morning. All I could think about was Marcy. I couldn't wait for the lunch bell to ring.

The minute it sounded I was halfway to the door.

"Hey, Zack," Danny called out. "You want me to save a seat for you in the cafeteria?"

"Sure, Danny," I answered. I wasn't going to the cafeteria. But I didn't want anyone to know that I was leaving school in the middle of the day.

When I was sure no one was watching, I slipped through the front door and burst outside.

I raced down Hawthorne Street to Canyon Drive.

I ran so hard I thought my lungs would burst. But I didn't stop. There was no time.

I reached Marcy's house in under five minutes.

And as I neared her front gate, I knew something was wrong.

The front door banged open and shut in the wind.

I sprinted up the walk.

Yes. Something was definitely wrong.

The glass in the big front window—it was totally shattered!

16

A man walked out the front door. A stranger with a dark brown beard. He wore a tool belt around his waist.

"Who are you?" I blurted. "Where are the Novis?"

"I'm from the glass company," the man told me. "I'm here to fix the window."

"Where is everyone?"

"The whole family left this morning," the man answered. He measured the new glass. "Some kind of family emergency."

"What kind of emergency?" I demanded.

"An emergency is all my boss told me," the man said.

"Do you know who broke the window?" I asked.

"No," he said, shaking his head. "But it's too bad. A window this big is hard to replace."

"Do you think it could have been some kind of explosion?" I asked.

"Could have been, I suppose," the man replied. "But when I checked the gas line, there was no sign of a leak. Kind of funny, isn't it?"

It wasn't funny at all.

I knew who was responsible.

Miss Gaunt.

What did she do to Marcy's family?

Suddenly I felt sick.

I wanted to go home.

But I couldn't. I had to warn my friends in school. I had to tell them how dangerous Miss Gaunt was.

I barely made it back to Shadyside Middle before the bell rang. Miss Gaunt brought the class to order.

I waited for a good time to write a note to Chris. But Miss Gaunt was staring at me every time I looked up. She kept her eyes on me all through geography and math.

"We'll spend the last hour on spelling," Miss Gaunt announced.

"Miss Prescott always teaches social studies on Tuesday afternoon," Tiffany complained.

"What is it you like so much about social studies, dear?"

"We were studying crop rotation," Tiffany said. "I liked reading about farmers—and how they keep feeding the soil to make things grow better."

"A sweet girl like you interested in dirt?" Miss Gaunt asked. "Why not wait till you're older to study nasty things like that?"

"Does that mean no social studies?" Tiffany asked.

"Not as long as I'm in charge," Miss Gaunt replied. "But how would you like to spell *rotation* for us?"

Tiffany sighed and walked up to the blackboard.

I knew I couldn't wait any longer.

It was time to spread the word about Miss Gaunt.

I ripped a sheet of paper from my notebook.

"Miss Gaunt is a ghost," I wrote. "I have proof. Be very carefull." I folded the paper and wrote Chris's name on the outside.

The seat in front of me was empty—Marcy's

71

seat. So I slipped the note to Debbie Steinford to my right. She's the class goody-goody, but I didn't think she'd tell Miss Gaunt.

Debbie shot me a dirty look, but she grabbed the note anyway. I watched her read Chris's name.

As Miss Gaunt watched Tiffany finish writing *rotation* on the board, Debbie passed the note to Ezra Goldstein in the row ahead of her.

Ezra passed the note to Danny Abernathy ahead of him.

Chris sat in the first row. I held my breath as Danny passed the note to him.

My eyes were glued to Chris as he unfolded the note under his desk.

He pushed his chair back.

Then he bent over to steal a better glimpse. When that didn't work, he spread the note out flat on top of his desk.

I saw him shake his head.

Then he turned around in his chair and flashed me that big stupid grin of his!

I checked the front of the class. Miss Gaunt had called Bobby Dreyfuss up to the board. He was trying to spell *artichoke*.

"A-R-T-A," Bobby spelled aloud as he wrote.

I heard someone snicker. A familiar snicker. Chris, of course.

"Christopher?" Miss Gaunt asked, looming over him. "What's that on you're desk?"

"It's nothing, Miss Gaunt," Chris said. He shoved the note in his pocket.

Bang! Bang! Bang!

Miss Gaunt slammed her pointer on his desk.

"Christopher!" she demanded. "Give me that note!"

17

Don't let me down, Chris! I thought. Just this once, keep your big mouth shut!

Chris reached into his pocket.

Throw it out the window, I begged silently. Or use that big mouth of yours to chew it up and swallow it.

If Miss Gaunt lays her bony hands on it, I'm in major trouble.

Chris held out the note. "This note, Miss Gaunt?" he asked timidly.

Thanks, Chris, I thought. Thanks a lot.

She snatched the note from him and read it carefully.

What if she recognizes my handwriting?

What if she realizes I wrote the note?

My mouth turned dry. I tried to swallow, but I couldn't. My hands began to shake so I hid them under my desk.

"A ghost," Miss Gaunt announced slowly. "Someone has accused *me* of being a ghost!"

Miss Gaunt paced slowly up and down the aisles. Studying each kid in the class.

"Can you imagine why someone would say that about me, Tiffany?" she asked.

Tiffany opened her mouth, then shut it. She shook her head.

Even Tiffany couldn't speak. And she's never afraid to talk.

"Can you imagine such a thing, Ezra?"

Ezra shook his head, too. He stared down at his desk.

"Well, one of you imagined it," Miss Gaunt said, her little voice growing higher and louder. "Or you wouldn't have written such a thing in the first place!"

Miss Gaunt stopped at Debbie's desk. "Did you write the note, Debbie?" she asked.

"No, Miss Gaunt," Debbie mumbled.

"Can you imagine why someone would say that

75

I am a ghost?" Miss Gaunt asked. "Is it because I am not as young as I used to be?"

"I don't know, Miss Gaunt," Debbie said. "You don't look so old to me."

Yeah, right! I thought. Miss Gaunt is at least two hundred years old! Can't anyone else see that?

"Thank you, my dear." Miss Gaunt patted Debbie on the shoulder.

Debbie shivered.

Miss Gaunt proceeded down the next aisle.

She was closing in on me.

I checked the clock. Five minutes left to the end of class.

Miss Gaunt paused at Danny's desk.

"Is it because I wear white?" Miss Gaunt asked him. "Is *that* why I have been called a ghost?"

"Maybe," Danny said, shrugging.

"Do you think it's nice to call someone a ghost?" Miss Gaunt asked.

"I would *never* call anyone a ghost, Miss Gaunt," Danny said. "That's for sure."

"That's because you are a very sensitive person," she said as she glided across the room to the next aisle. "You would never be so unkind."

I glanced at the clock again.

Only three minutes left before the final bell.

Maybe she won't make it to me, I prayed.

"You can't imagine what it's like to be a substitute teacher," Miss Gaunt continued. "You hardly know a soul. You feel so alone. Then someone starts spreading unkind rumors." She spun around and glared at Bobby Dreyfuss. "How do you think that makes me feel?"

"Not good, I guess," Bobby answered, his lips quivering.

Miss Gaunt slammed her pointer down on his desk so hard he jumped out of his seat.

"Exactly!" Miss Gaunt screeched. "Let me tell you, boys and girls, gossip is not a pretty thing. Gossip is cruel. And what do we do to people who are cruel?"

Bobby stared up at her. "I-I guess we punish them," he stuttered.

"Punish them!" Miss Gaunt's voice grew even louder. "Very good, Bobby. That's exactly what we do. We punish them!"

I started to break out into a cold sweat. Tiny beads of perspiration dripped down my forehead.

If Miss Gaunt looks at me now, she'll know.

She'll know I wrote that note.

She'll know I said she was a ghost.

I checked the clock.

One minute left.

One minute until the bell.

"Don't worry, boys and girls," Miss Guant said, the tone of her voice suddenly soft and gentle. "I am not going to pursue this matter any further. I just want everyone to know that whoever wrote this note has hurt my feelings deeply. Very deeply."

The bell rang.

I could hardly believe my luck.

She didn't find out that I wrote the note!

I scooped up my backpack and raced to the door—and felt an icy hand squeeze my shoulder.

Miss Gaunt's hand.

"Zachariah," she said sweetly. "I am afraid I have to ask you to stay after class today!"

18

"**B**ut I-I've got to get home, Miss Gaunt," I stammered. "My mom's expecting me."

"This won't take but a moment, dear," she said.

A moment was way too long to be alone with a ghost.

But I didn't have any choice.

"Sorry," Chris mouthed on his way out the door.

Tiffany smiled sympathetically. But most of the other kids didn't even glance at me. They rushed out with their eyes glued to the floor.

When the last kid left, Miss Gaunt shut the

door. The quiet little click the lock made sent a chill down my spine.

Then she turned toward me. "You're frightened, aren't you, Zachariah?"

I nodded slowly.

"Lots of things scare you. Don't they, Zachariah?" she said. "That's why you bought that book *Power Kids,* isn't it?"

"N-no one knows about that," I stammered. "How could—"

"Oh, I noticed you in the bookstore," Miss Gaunt said. "It was the day before I started here. I visited town. To stretch my legs. And get the cobwebs out of my hair, so to speak. And I couldn't help thinking, 'What a fine boy. He'd be perfect.'"

Perfect for what? I wondered. *Perfect for what?*

"And here I was—just about to take over another class. But as soon as I spotted you, I knew I had to arrange for your teacher to come down with a cold. A nasty cold. It was naughty of me, I suppose, but I just couldn't resist!"

"Y-you made Miss Prescott sick?" I asked.

"I'm sorry to say I did. But I knew I *had* to be *your* teacher!"

Miss Gaunt approached her desk. She unfolded the note and read it again.

80

Maybe I can tell her the note was a joke, I thought. A stupid Halloween joke.

No. There's no way she'd believe me.

"What can I say, Zachariah?" Miss Gaunt asked. "Except that today I am very disappointed in you."

I was trapped!

And scared.

Really scared.

What was Miss Gaunt going to do to me?

She continued on. "You need to work on your spelling, dear." She held the note up in front of me. *"Careful* has only one *l*. Fortunately for you, your error won't influence your final grade."

Spelling! She wanted to talk to me about spelling?

"You're right, Miss Gaunt," I said quickly. "I'll go straight home and start studying."

"That won't be necessary, Zachariah."

Keep her talking, I told myself. Maybe Chris will wonder what's taking me so long. And he'll come back.

"Um. Is that how you knew I wrote the note?" I asked. "Because of the spelling?"

"Not entirely," Miss Gaunt said. "You followed me to the cemetery yesterday. You discovered the

81

grave—and the truth. So you see—you were the only one who could have written that note."

"Marcy could have!" I blurted.

"Well, we don't have to worry about her anymore. Do we?"

"What did you do to her?" I croaked. I was so frightened now, I nearly choked on my own words. "Where—where is she?"

"You know, Zachariah, I do not understand why you had to drag her along. She could have ruined everything."

I glanced behind me. Could I jump through one of the windows? I wondered.

Miss Gaunt placed the note on her desk and reached into a drawer. She lifted out a silver-wrapped box, topped with a shiny black bow.

"Ah!" she cried. "Enough about Marcy. I have a present for you."

What would a ghost give as a present? I didn't want to find out.

"That's okay, Miss Gaunt. You don't have to give me anything."

Could I push past her and escape?

"Nonsense, Zachariah," Miss Gaunt replied. "I want to give you a present. After all, *you* are my favorite student."

"What about Debbie Steinford?" The words

82

flew out of my mouth. "All the teachers love Debbie!"

"No. No. Zachariah. This is for you. To open later."

She shoved the package into my backpack. I didn't know what was in it—and I didn't want to know.

Miss Gaunt scooped up the note from her desk. She tore it up and threw the shreds in the wastebasket.

"No one believed your silly note," she said. "Which is certainly a nice piece of luck for me. I suspect the principal wouldn't be very happy if he knew I was a ghost!"

"I promise I won't tell anyone. You're a wonderful teacher, Miss Gaunt. I won't do anything to get you in trouble!"

Miss Gaunt smiled at me. "Do you really think I am a wonderful teacher, Zachariah?"

"Definitely. I've learned tons from you," I told her.

"Yes. You are correct. I am a wonderful teacher. And it's just not fair," Miss Gaunt said. "Can you imagine that I can leave my grave only once every ten years—the week before Halloween? That's not very often, is it?"

"No, Miss Gaunt," I agreed. "That's not very often."

How was I going to escape? I had to find a way out!

"And what's worse," she continued, "is that on the stroke of twelve on Halloween night I must return to my grave. Which is why I try to make the most of my time. I love every second of it, too. But especially the Halloween party. Do you like Halloween parties, Zachariah?"

"Oh, sure, Miss Gaunt," I answered nervously. "Who doesn't like Halloween parties?"

If I ran for it, would she try to catch me?

"Do you know what the highlight of the party is for me?" she asked.

I shook my head.

"The highlight is when I pick my favorite student," she said.

"What do you pick a student for?" My voice cracked.

"You know, don't you?" Miss Gaunt said. "That's why you're so frightened, isn't it?"

"I don't know anything. I don't know what you want with me. I don't want to know, Miss Gaunt. Please, let me go home," I begged.

She's never going to let me leave!

"Allow me to explain," Miss Gaunt began.

"Every ten years I select one student to take back with me," she said.

"Back with you?" I gasped. "Back where?"

"Why, back to the grave, of course," she said. "Back to the grave—to become a ghost like me. And then I will be able to teach them—forever!"

"I don't want to go with you, Miss Gaunt! I want to stay here in Shadyside!"

"But I need you, Zachariah," she said. "You're so much brighter than the others."

"I am not brighter," I protested. "I'm not good at decimals. I'm not good at spelling. You just said so yourself!"

"Ah, but you guessed what other children couldn't even imagine about me."

"No!" I shouted. "I won't go!"

"Oh, Zachariah." Miss Gaunt pouted. "Aren't you even a tiny bit pleased?"

I didn't trust myself to speak. I was afraid if I opened my mouth I would start screaming. And never stop.

I ran to the door.

I twisted the lock.

As I swung the door open, Miss Gaunt called after me. "Halloween . . . tomorrow, Zachariah. Midnight! To join our dark, dark world—of ghosts."

19

Her grave!

She's planning to take me back to her grave! And make me a ghost!

I ran from the classroom.

I pounded down the hall. I slammed through the school's big double doors. And jumped off the top step, flying to the ground. Then I raced down Hawthorne as fast as I could.

The white strips of cloth hanging from the oak tree on the corner whipped across my face. I didn't slow down.

Jack-o'-lanterns leered at my from every porch. Jack-o'-lanterns for Halloween.

I slipped on some wet leaves and nearly fell.

Don't stop, I told myself. Just get home. Get home and don't come out until Halloween is over.

I ran so hard I thought my chest would explode.

Home, I thought every time one of my feet hit the cement.

Home, home, home, home.

I turned a corner. I was nearly there!

I dashed past the neighbors' houses. Then I cut across my lawn and charged up to the door.

It was locked.

I shoved my hands into my pockets. Empty. What did I do with my key?

I hammered on the door. "Let me in!" I screamed.

What if Miss Gaunt realizes I'm never coming out of the house? What if she's on her way here? What if she decides to take me back to her grave—now?

I beat on the door with both fists.

"Who is it?" I heard my brother, Kevin, call in a high voice.

"Kevin, let me in!" I hollered.

"We don't need anything. Have a nice day!" Kevin trilled.

"Kevin, open it! Now! Or I'm calling Mom!"

"Mom's not home!" Kevin yelled back.

I rammed my shoulder against the door the way they do in cop shows. I didn't care if I broke the door down. I had to get inside.

I threw myself at the door again. And as I did, Kevin opened it. I soared into the hallway.

Kevin laughed like an idiot.

I slammed the door and locked it. I slid the chain in place.

Kevin leaned against the wall. Watching. "I knew Halloween would drive you completely insane some year," he told me.

I ignored him. I ran around to the back door and locked it. Then I made sure every window was locked.

Are ghosts like vampires? I wondered. Do they have to be invited in before they can enter a house?

I hurried upstairs and checked all the windows up there, too. I triple-checked my own window. Then I threw myself facedown on my bed.

My backpack opened and something slid out.

Miss Gaunt's present.

I threw it on the floor.

And stared at it.

Miss Gaunt had wrapped it carefully. The corners were nice and smooth. The black bow was arranged just so.

What is in it? I wondered. Some gross dead thing? Or something worse? Something alive? Is it safe to have it in the house?

I sat up and nudged the present with my toe. I didn't hear anything. I gave the package a kick. Nothing.

I knelt down and ran my fingers over the silver paper. It felt like a book.

I slowly tore away a corner of the paper. I was right. A book.

I inhaled deeply.

A book.

That's not so bad.

I ripped the rest of the paper away.

My stomach lurched when I read the front cover.

The title said: *The Book of the Dead.*

20

The Book of the Dead.

I touched the cover with the tip of one finger. I expected it to feel cold—like Miss Gaunt.

But it didn't. It felt warm.

I opened it up—and spotted my name! I slammed the book shut.

I'm throwing this thing out, I decided. There's nothing in *The Book of the Dead* that I need to know. At least not for a long, *long* time.

I grabbed the book and tossed it in the wastebasket.

Wait, I thought. Maybe I should read the part that has my name in it.

I flipped open the cover. It was an inscription and it said:

> For Zachariah,
> Welcome!
> Your teacher *forever,*
> Evangeline Gaunt.

No way, I thought. No way!

I noticed again how warm the book felt. It started to pulse under my fingertips. As if it were alive.

I flung it back into the trash.

Don't flip out, I told myself. Don't flip out. You just have to make it through one more day. At midnight on Halloween this will all be over.

I headed back downstairs. Usually I avoid Kevin—especially when Mom and Dad aren't around to referee. But I was terrified, and I didn't want to be by myself.

Chris called on the phone about a million times, but I made Kevin tell him I wasn't feeling well.

After dinner I hung around my parents. It would be pretty hard for Miss Gaunt to drag me away from them, I figured. I could tell my parents thought I was acting weird, but they didn't say anything about it.

91

After my favorite TV show ended, Mom said it was time for bed.

Sleep. Upstairs. Alone.

"Can't I stay up a little bit longer?" I begged.

"Sorry, Zach," she replied. "You know it's a school night."

I practically crawled up the stairs. But when I reached my room, I sprinted inside and jumped between the sheets of my bed. Then I tugged the covers up to my chin.

Every time I closed my eyes, I imagined myself lying in a grave. With thousands of swollen worms wriggling underneath me.

So I stayed up all night.

Trying to come up with a plan.

A plan to stay home from school.

My life depended on it!

The next morning I leaped out of bed.

I slipped into the bathroom and closed the door. I turned on the hot water in the bathtub and let it run. I wanted the bathroom to be nice and steamy.

After about five minutes my pajamas began to stick to me. Now I appeared all sweaty.

I drenched a washcloth in hot tap water, and I wrung it out. Then I pressed it to my forehead. Instant fever!

I bolted downstairs before my fake fever cooled.

"You'd better get dressed, honey," Mom said as I entered the kitchen. "You don't want to be late for school."

Yes, I do, I thought. I want to be so late that I won't arrive there till tomorrow.

She held out a glass of orange juice. I pushed it away. I sagged into my chair. "I don't feel so well," I moaned.

Kevin wandered in and plopped down across the table. He snagged my juice.

Mom placed her hand on my forehead. "You do feel a little warm," she commented.

"Check his pulse," Kevin said. "Just to see if he has one."

"Be nice," Mom said. "Your poor brother isn't feeling well. You go back to bed, honey. I'll bring you something to eat in a few minutes."

Before Mom started talking about calling the doctor, I darted upstairs. I turned on the TV and tuned into some lame game shows.

But I watched the clock more than I watched the television—counting down the time until I was safe from Miss Gaunt.

At four o'clock I couldn't decide whether I should be relieved—or more scared than ever. The

Halloween party was over. But it was hours until midnight.

And now that school was out, Miss Gaunt could be anywhere. I had eight more hours to go. Eight long hours.

The next two hours I didn't even pretend to watch TV. I stared at the clock. Gazing at the seconds and minutes ticking away.

Mom popped into my room at six o'clock. She felt my forehead. "Good!" she exclaimed. No more fever! Are you ready for Halloween?" she asked.

I nearly gasped. "I-uh-thought I wasn't allowed out today."

"Wouldn't you like to greet the trick-or-treaters at the door?"

"Oh, sure," I answered. Boy, was I relieved.

"Great costume, Zack," Kevin called as I came down the stairs.

"I'm not wearing a costume," I snapped.

"Sure you are. You're the Big Pain!" Kevin laughed. "You'll do anything to get out of Halloween, won't you?" he demanded. "You can fool Mom, but you can't fool me."

I ignored him. He shuffled off to the kitchen.

The doorbell rang.

I grabbed the bowl of candy Mom had set out on the hall table.

I pulled open the door.

"Trick or treat! Trick or treat!"

A bunch of little kids perched on the porch. I could see their mothers waiting for them on the sidewalk. I dropped candy in each of their bags.

The doorbell rang again.

"Trick or treat! Trick or treat!"

A Martian, a dinosaur, and a ballerina appeared.

I handed out the candy—and even pretended to be frightened of the tiny dinosaur. The kids giggled as I closed the door.

The doorbell rang again.

It's going to be a busy night, I thought. Halloween will be over before I know it!

I opened the door.

Only one person stood there.

"Trick or treat, Zachariah!"

Miss Gaunt!

21

I froze in the doorway. I stared at the white gauzy gown. The white gloves. The veil.

It was Miss Gaunt! She had come for me!

"You can't come in!" I shouted. "I won't let you."

"Zack, honey?" Mom ran in from the kitchen. "Is everything okay?"

I clutched Mom's arm. "It's Miss Gaunt. My substitute teacher!" I cried. "Don't let her take me away!"

"Let me feel your forehead," Mom said. "Maybe you do have a fever."

"She wants to kidnap me!" I screamed as Mom lifted her hand to my forehead. "She is going to kill me and make me live in the graveyard!"

"But, Zack—" Mom started.

"Save me, Mom," I interrupted. "You've got to save me!"

"But, Zack," Mom said again. "Miss Gaunt isn't here. It's just . . ."

Then I heard the laughter. I turned. Miss Gaunt had lifted her veil. And underneath—it wasn't Miss Gaunt at all.

It was Chris. And now he was doubled over, laughing his head off.

"Did I really look like her?" Chris asked between gasps of laughter.

"You know you look *exactly* like her!" I said. "You did this on purpose. Just to scare me!"

"I thought it would be funny," Chris said, still chuckling. "Besides, I didn't come over just to scare you. I came to see how you were feeling."

"Why, isn't that nice of him?" Mom said. "Would you like a treat, Chris?"

"Thanks, Mrs. Pepper," Chris said. He strolled over to the treat table. Once Mom headed back to the kitchen, he started cramming candy bars into his pillowcase.

"Anyone notice I was sick?" I asked Chris. "Besides you, I mean?"

"Miss Gaunt noticed. And boy, did she seem upset. She really *is* nuts about you."

"Upset how?" I asked. "Was she, um, sad-upset—or angry-upset?"

"More like brokenhearted-upset," Chris said. "I have to admit, it was a little weird."

Chris shook his pillowcase to make room for more candy. Then he continued. "Anyway, Miss Gaunt told us that Miss Prescott will be back on Monday. Miss Gaunt said she was really sorry to leave without saying goodbye to you and Marcy."

"Has anybody heard from Marcy?" I asked anxiously.

"Nah. But I passed her house coming here. The window is fixed. I'm sure she'll be home soon."

That's what you think, I muttered under my breath.

"What?" Chris asked. His pillowcase was full now, and he was getting ready to leave.

I knew Chris would never believe me. But I had to try to convince him. "Miss Gaunt is a ghost!" I shouted. "And she's done something horrible to Marcy and her family."

"Oh, right," Chris said sarcastically. "I read your stupid note."

"She really is a ghost. And she got rid of Marcy because we saw her grave."

"What grave?"

"Her grave. Miss Gaunt's grave! It said 'Born 1769. Died 1845.' "

"You saw *her* grave?" Chris asked. "With her name on it?"

"Yes!" I answered with a sigh of relief. It looked as if Chris was finally beginning to believe me.

Chris set his pillowcase on the floor. "Hmmm. I know. It was probably her great-great-great grandmother's grave."

"But the grave was empty!" I cried.

"That doesn't prove she's a ghost, Zack."

"Look, Chris. Marcy's gone. Gone because we saw Miss Gaunt's grave. Because we know the truth. Miss Gaunt is a ghost. Why won't you believe me? She told me that she wants to take me back with her to the graveyard. Tonight. Why would she say that if she weren't a ghost?"

"For special math tutoring?" Chris asked, starting to laugh again.

"No! NO! NO!" I screamed. "She wants to turn me into a ghost, too."

"Well, maybe you won't be afraid of ghosts anymore—once you're one of them." Chris laughed so hard now he had to clutch his sides.

"What's all the laughing about?" Mom asked, coming up beside me. "Are you feeling better?"

"No, Mom. I'm not feeling better. In fact, I feel a lot worse," I said, glaring at Chris.

"Well, why don't you go up to bed?" Mom replied. "Get some rest. I have to go next door for a few minutes. Come on, Chris. I'll walk you out."

Chris and Mom left. I practically slammed the door behind them. I noticed Chris's pillowcase on the floor. He had left it behind. Well, too bad. He wasn't getting it back.

I started up the stairs to bed when the doorbell rang again. "Kevin!" I yelled for my brother. "Get the door!"

No answer.

Great. I muttered. Kevin never does anything around here. I'll be answering the door all night.

The doorbell rang again.

"Okay. Okay. I'm coming."

As I approached the door, I could hear the shouts of the trick-or-treaters outside. I wished Halloween were over.

I yanked the door open. It was Chris.

"Forget it! I'm not giving you your stupid candy!" I shouted.

"Candy? I didn't come for candy, Zachariah. I came for you!"

It was Miss Gaunt.

The real Miss Gaunt!

22

~~~

Miss Gaunt reached out a gloved hand and grasped me tightly by the wrist.

"No!" I shrieked. "I won't go! I don't want to be a ghost!"

"It doesn't matter what you want!" she said calmly. "Don't you understand that?"

She didn't sound like an old lady anymore. Her voice was strong—and mean. And her grip was like iron.

She yanked me forward, dragging me toward the front door. I grabbed the doorknob to the front closet. I tried to pull myself back.

"Help!" I screamed. "Help!"

I heard footsteps coming down the stairs. Kevin.

As soon as he appeared, Miss Gaunt loosened her grip. "Hello, there," Miss Gaunt said. "I'm Zachariah's substitute teacher. I stopped by to invite him to a Halloween party."

"Don't believe her!" I cried. "Our class Halloween party was this afternoon!"

Kevin studied Miss Gaunt. "Hey, that's a really cool costume," he finally said. Then he turned to me. "Zack, you're pathetic. You'd say anything to skip Halloween."

"Actually, Zack is right. Our class Halloween party was this afternoon," Miss Gaunt said sweetly. "But some of the children thought it would be nice to have another one tonight. It would be a shame for Zack to miss that one, too."

"Don't let her take me!" I shrieked. "She's going to force me into the graveyard and turn me into a ghost—just like her!"

"Are you really going to turn Zack into a ghost?" Kevin laughed.

"I promised him I would," Miss Gaunt said. "I think it's important for grown-ups to live up to their promises. Don't you?"

"Well, have a great time at the party," Kevin said, heading up the stairs.

I tried to run after him, but Miss Gaunt was way too fast for me. She lunged for my arm. Her grip felt strong enough to crush my bones.

She jerked me down our front path onto the sidewalk. As we passed our neighbor's house, I screamed. "Mom! Come out! Mom!" But she couldn't hear me.

My shoes scraped the sidewalk as Miss Gaunt yanked on my arm. I thought she was going to pull it right out of its socket.

My eyes searched the street for help. Two kids dressed as aliens were approaching us.

"Help! Help!" I screamed.

"Oooh! Oooh!" they giggled.

"She's going to turn me into a ghost!" I cried.

"Really?" one of the aliens asked.

"I'm certainly going to do my best," Miss Gaunt replied in her thin, breathy voice.

The kids laughed and jogged up the steps to the next house.

Miss Gaunt gripped my arm tighter. Practically lifting me off the ground. We glided down the street.

"Help me!" I begged two masked bandits. "She's kidnapping me!"

But the bandits laughed, too.

We turned down Fear Street.

There were no trick-or-treaters. No one out. The street was deserted. The air—perfectly still. Nothing moved.

A dim light shone through the window of a house every now and then. But mostly it was dark. And creepy. As creepy as the night Marcy and I followed Miss Gaunt on our bikes.

"Miss Gaunt, please don't do this. Please," I begged, struggling to free myself.

"But I have to, Zachariah," Miss Gaunt answered. "You're such a good student. I want to teach you—forever."

I tried to rip my arm from Miss Gaunt's grasp. She clamped down harder. Nothing could stop her. She glided faster down Fear Street, dragging me behind.

We reached a corner. And turned.

We had come to the Fear Street Cemetery.

"Home, Zachariah," Miss Gaunt announced. "Home at last!"

23

"No way!" I screamed. "I'm not going in there.
You're never going to get away with this!"

"But I already have!" she cackled.

I twisted in Miss Gaunt's grip. But she had the
strength of a wrestler.

I opened my mouth wide and sank my teeth into
the folds of her gauzy sleeve. I heard a sickening
crunch. Her arm snapped. I had broken her bone.
In the moonlight I glimpsed the jagged edge
poking through her sleeve. But it didn't seem to
matter. Her grip was as strong as ever.

"Don't do that again," Miss Gaunt warned.

"You don't want to make me cross, do you, Zachariah?"

We entered the Fear Street Cemetery. And I spotted a familiar-looking man. It was Mr. Sangfwad from Shop Till You Drop (Dead!).

What was he doing in the cemetery? Could he save me?

"Mr. Sangfwad!" I yelled. "Help me! Mr. Sangfwad!"

Mr. Sangfwad turned toward me. But he made no effort to help. He didn't seem to recognize me.

"It's me!" I screamed. "Zack Pepper. I was in your store the other day."

"Ah," he said as he moved closer. And then I realized why Mr. Sangfwad didn't know who I was. His eyes were gone! Two empty sockets stared out into the darkness.

Mr. Sangfwad was a ghost, too!

"Welcome to our little party," he said. Then he wiped some drool from his bony chin.

"Let me go," I begged. "I want to go home."

"But the party's just begun," Miss Gaunt crooned.

"I don't want to be at this party!" I cried out. "I don't belong here."

"But you're the life of the party!" Mr. Sangfwad cackled. "At least until midnight."

"Wh-what happens at midnight?" I asked.

Mr. Sangfwad placed his face close to mine. I tried to shrink back from his foul breath. But Miss Gaunt held me firmly.

His lips brushed my ear as he whispered into it. "At midnight you will become the un-life of the party. You will turn into a ghost—just like us."

Then Mr. Sangfwad threw back his head and shrieked—like a madman.

"I don't want to be a ghost!" I cried over his awful howls.

"I am afraid Zachariah isn't in a party mood tonight," Miss Gaunt said. "It was nice to see you, Mr. Sangfwad. But we must be on our way."

Miss Gaunt tugged me deeper into the grave-yard. But we could still hear Mr. Sangfwad's shrieks echoing all around us.

The air grew colder as we plunged deeper still. The graves in this part of the cemetery were older and smaller. I tried to focus on them, but we were moving too fast. They passed in a blur.

And then, finally, we stopped.

At a grave.

The open grave Marcy and I had seen before.

Only this time, a coffin rested within it.

And the lid was open. Waiting.

Waiting for us.

24

"**Y**ou can't make me go down there," I screeched. "I won't let you!"

"Oh, Zachariah," Miss Gaunt said. "It's no use fighting. Can't you see that?"

"But I don't want to go with you!" I pleaded. "I want to go home."

"But this *is* your home," Miss Gaunt said. "Come, Zachariah. It is time."

"No!" I screamed. "I won't! I can't!"

I pushed back with all my strength. The force set me free! My head hit the ground with a thud. Right next to the open grave.

I gazed up. Miss Gaunt was calmly peeling off one of her white gloves.

I inched my way back. Back. Sliding along the wet grass.

Miss Gaunt moved forward. Slowly. Then her arm shot out. And before I could dodge away, her bare bony fingers were digging deep into my shoulder.

She lifted me up with one hand. "Come with me, Zachariah," she whispered.

My strength faded. My legs began to tremble. Step by step, my feet slipped across the grass as Miss Gaunt pulled me forward.

I hovered at the edge of the grave now. Peering down. Down at the open coffin.

Miss Gaunt stood beside me. "Welcome home, Zachariah," she said, with a soft cackle. And then she shoved me. One quick hard shove.

And before I knew it, I was falling.

Falling into Miss Gaunt's grave.

Into the open coffin.

25

"Help!" I screamed. "Help!"

I landed facedown in the coffin.

"Comfy, isn't it?" Miss Gaunt purred from above.

I scrambled to my feet. I threw myself against the side of the grave, struggling to climb out. I clutched at the dirt—trying to pull myself up. But the ancient soil crumbled beneath my grip.

"Help!" I screamed again. "Someone, help me!"

"My goodness, Zachariah," Miss Gaunt said. "Please. Not so loud. You're going to wake up the dead." And then she laughed. Not her wispy laugh—a deep, cruel laugh.

112

I reached up. Groping at the wall of the grave. My fingers wrapped around a thick tree root. I dug my hands into the dirt and grasped the root tightly. I began to hoist myself out.

"Save your strength," Miss Gaunt called down. "You can't escape. It's much too late for that. It's almost midnight."

"No!" I cried out. "I'm not staying here with you!"

"I'm afraid you have no choice, dear," she said, kneeling beside the grave, peering down. "Just think how lovely it's going to be. Think of all the time we'll have together. All the things I'll be able to teach you. After all, I am a wonderful teacher."

I reached up—to shove Miss Gaunt back. But my hand caught her veil—ripping it away.

"What have you done?" Miss Gaunt shrieked. She jerked up and turned to search the ground for her veil.

I clutched the tree root tightly. I jammed one foot into the dirt. Then I pushed up with the other foot with all my strength.

I sprang up.

I held on to the tree root with one hand and reached out for the grave's opening with the other. Then I pulled myself out.

I jumped quickly to my feet.

Miss Gaunt whirled around.

And her face was gone!

No flesh.

Just a bony skull holding a few wisps of gray hair. And worms. Slimy purple worms. Crawling in and out of the sockets where her eyes should have been.

I choked back a scream. My hands flew to my eyes, covering them.

"Look at me, Zachariah," Miss Gaunt ordered.

"I can't!" I shrieked, gasping for breath.

"You must," she commanded harshly. Then her voice softened. "You must, Zachariah. You must. Because in a few minutes, you will look exactly like this, too."

My hands floated away from my eyes. Moving by themselves—controlled by Miss Gaunt. I stared into her horrifying face.

"You can't get away from me!" she said. "I'm never going to let you go. Never!"

I glanced down at her hands. Her raw, bony fingers twitched in the moonlight.

Then they shot out and curled around my neck.

"Let me go!" I shrieked. I tried to pry her fingers from my throat, but she was too strong.

I struggled hard. She shoved me back. My foot

dangled over the open grave. I was losing my balance.

In the distance the town clock began to strike midnight. One . . . Two . . . Three . . .

Footsteps. It was difficult to tell, but I thought I heard footsteps.

Miss Gaunt heard them, too.

She snapped her head up. She peered over my shoulder. Her body stiffened.

She lifted a bony finger and pointed. "Wh-who is . . ."

What could possibly scare *her* this much?

I whirled around.

It was another Miss Gaunt!

26

Another Miss Gaunt—with big white high-tops peeking out from under her white dress. Chris!

I was never so glad to see him in my life!

"Come on! Help me!" I cried out. I grabbed Miss Gaunt's spindly arm and swung her into the coffin.

Then I slammed the lid down and jumped on top of the coffin. It rumbled underneath me.

"Come on, Chris! Help me hold this thing down, now!"

The clock continued to chime. Seven . . . Eight . . .

Chris jumped down next to me. His "Miss

Gaunt" veil flew up in his face as the wind began
to blow. Then the whole ground shook.

The coffin lid jerked open and a howling wind
escaped from inside the casket!

We slammed the lid down again. It snapped
open once more—with a force that sent dirt
flinging from the grave.

"Hold it down!" I screamed. "Hold it down!"

Nine . . .

The wind howled in our ears. Soil and rocks
whipped around us. Pelting us.

There were only seconds left until midnight.
Seconds before Miss Gaunt returned to the world
of ghosts. Seconds before I was safe—finally.

Ten . . .

The coffin lid wrenched open and a bony hand
shot out! It grabbed me by the ankle.

"Oh, no! Not now!" I shrieked. I kicked wildly
to free myself—before it was too late. But the
harder I struggled, the tighter her grip grew.

Eleven . . .

I was slipping—slipping into the coffin. Slipping away—forever.

Twelve!

A jagged bolt of lightning sliced through the
sky. It pierced the ground next to the grave.

Miss Gaunt's bony hand suddenly dropped

from my leg. I watched in horror as it shriveled up and shrank back into the coffin.

Then the wind died. And the dirt storm settled. The cemetery grew silent.

It was midnight. Halloween had ended.

I didn't realize I had been holding my breath. I let out a long sigh.

Chris and I pulled ourselves out of the grave.

"Thanks," I said, turning toward him. The color had completely drained from his face. Even his freckles were pale.

"I-I was walking by the cemetery," he stammered. "I heard someone screaming for help. It sounded like you."

"You showed up just in time!" I cried.

"I-I can't believe it," he said. "Miss Gaunt really was a ghost!"

Even in the moonlight, there was no mistaking the look on Chris's face. The look of horror. For the first time all week, I smiled.

27

"**I** decided to let you sleep in," Mom said when I walked into the kitchen Saturday morning. "I was afraid you didn't get enough sleep last night."

"I feel terrific, Mom," I said, chugging my juice.

"Well, I don't approve of your teacher keeping you out that late," Mom said. "And I'm going to talk to her about it."

"I don't think you can," I said. "Yesterday was her last day."

"I'll find her number in the telephone book," Mom replied. "What is her last name? Gaunt. Right?"

"Uh-huh," I said. "But I have a feeling her number is unlisted."

I grabbed a piece of toast and headed for the door. "See you later."

I raced over to Marcy's house. The window was fixed, but the house appeared deserted. I knocked on the door.

It slowly creaked open. And there she was!

"Marcy!" I cried. "You're here!"

Marcy stepped outside. She closed the door behind her very carefully. "Dad said not to slam the door," Marcy explained. "That's how he broke the window the other day."

Well, that explains one thing, I thought.

"Marcy, where *were* you?" I asked.

We sat on her front lawn. "It was the weirdest thing," she began. "After you rode off Thursday, I ran into the house. And Mom was on the phone. When she hung up she said we had to leave for my grandmother's house upstate right away."

"Did she say why?" I asked.

"Yes. She said Grandma was very sick."

"What's weird about that?" I asked.

"Wait," Marcy said, holding up her hand. Then she continued. "We jumped in the car. Dad drove all night. We reached Grandma's house Friday morning. Grandma ran out of the house to meet us. And she was fine!"

"Pretty fast recovery, huh?" I said.

"No, Zack. *That* was the weird part. Grandma said she never called. She didn't know what Mom was talking about."

"I bet Miss Gaunt did it!" I cried. Then I told Marcy all about Halloween.

Marcy couldn't believe what had happened. "Well, at least no one will ever tease you about ghosts again."

"Yeah," I agreed. Then I jumped up. "Hey, there's Chris!" I waved him over.

"Chris, I was just telling Marcy all about Halloween."

"What about it?" Chris said.

Chris was playing it cool. I guess he couldn't bear the thought that I was right for once.

"Oh, just about Miss Gaunt being a ghost and all."

"Miss Gaunt? A ghost? Are you starting that again?"

"What do you mean?" I shouted in Chris's face. "Of course Miss Gaunt was a ghost. You saw her. You were in the cemetery with me! You were scared to death!"

121

Chris laughed. "Me? Scared? No way. That ghost stuff is strictly in *your* dreams, Zack. Not mine."

Chris didn't remember a thing. It was the last of Miss Gaunt's ghostly magic.

On Monday morning I walked to school by myself. When the school came into view, I reached into my backpack and pulled out Chris's snake. It was hard to believe—only a couple of weeks ago this thing terrified me.

I held the snake to my face and felt its slimy texture on my skin.

"Oshee ma terr hoom," I chanted softly. "Kubal den skaya!" It was one of the chants I had memorized from the book I rescued from the garbage—*The Book of the Dead*.

The rubber snake came to life. It slithered through my fingers. I patted it gently.

"So, Chris isn't scared of anything," I said to myself. "We'll see."

I ran up the stairs to Shadyside Middle School and raced down the hall. I learned a lot from Miss Gaunt, I thought as the snake slithered happily down into my backpack. Miss Gaunt was a wonderful teacher.

GHOSTS of FEAR STREET ®

STAY AWAY FROM THE TREE HOUSE

For as long as I can remember, I've wanted to see a ghost. I don't think I'm asking a lot. I just want to meet one honest-to-goodness, terrifying, transparent, terrible ghost. Then I'll shut up about it.

It's really not fair that I haven't seen a ghost before this. Other kids around here have seen at least *one* spooky, hideous thing in their lives. But not me, Dylan Brown. No way. Even though I live on Fear Street, the scariest place in the world, my life has been the most boring, ordinary, totally ghost-free life in history.

But I had a feeling today was going to be different. Today was the day I was finally going to see a ghost.

Why?

Because it was definitely ghost weather today.

The morning had started out bright and sunny—a perfect spring day. But by the afternoon, heavy clouds rolled in and the sky turned dark and gloomy. Just the kind of weather ghosts like—don't you think?

Well, that's what I was thinking as I leaned back in Dad's squashy old green chair. I put the book I was reading in my lap and stared out the window. A strong wind was blowing now. And the tree branches in the front yard trembled.

Fear Street looks good and creepy today, I thought, pressing my nose against the window. *Perfect for finally meeting a creature from another world. So . . . where is it?*

It wasn't in my yard—that was obvious.

I stared left and right—into our neighbors' yards.

Nope. Nothing there.

Then I peered down the street.

And spotted something. A shadow. Darting out from behind a low bush. My heart raced—just a little.

Don't get your hopes up, I told myself. *It's probably Pokey, the neighbor's smelly old dog.*

I stared harder. It was still there. Hovering.

Maybe, just maybe, it isn't Pokey, I thought.

Maybe it's the ghost I've been waiting for my whole life.

Yes. This could be it. "Don't just sit here," I said out loud. "Go outside and check."

I closed my book—*The Book of Amazing All-True Ghost Stories*—and pictured myself marching across the street. I wasn't exactly sure how you were supposed to talk to a ghost. But I thought I'd say something like, "Come out now, Oh Unearthly One. Show yourself to me—Dylan S. Brown, fearless hunter of ghosts!"

A shadowy thing would ooze out from behind the bushes. As I stared at it, the thing would transform into a giant ghost-monster with glistening, knife-sharp teeth.

I wouldn't move an inch. No, I, Dylan S. Brown, ghost hunter would—

Bam!

Something behind me—something hard and icy—slammed down on my shoulder.

I leaped out of the chair, tripped over my own feet, and crashed to the floor.

"Get a grip, Dylan." My big brother stood over me, laughing his stupid head off. He held a Coke can in his hand—the cold can he had bashed into my shoulder. "You're turning into a bigger wimp every day."

I wanted to punch him in the knee. I had a great

3

shot at it from my spot on the floor. But if I did, Steve would probably tickle me.

He knows how much I hate being tickled. And he wouldn't stop until I promised to make his bed for a week.

So I didn't do anything—except sigh. Then I shoved myself up and said, "You surprised me, that's all." Boy, did that sound lame.

"Yeah, right," Steve replied. He took his baseball cap off his head and ran his fingers through his blond hair, smoothing it. Then he put the cap back on.

"I'll make you a deal. You do my paper route in the morning, and I won't tell everyone in school what a wimp you are."

I knew Steve wouldn't tell anyone. He could be a pain at home. But at school he always backed me up. "No way," I answered. "I'm not getting up at five in the morning to deliver your papers. And I'm not taking your turn doing the dishes or taking out the garbage either. So don't try to make another deal. Besides, I have better things to do."

"Oh, yeah. Like what?" Steve asked.

I pointed outside at the gloomy street. "Even you can see it's the perfect kind of day for finding a ghost."

"Oh, give me a break," Steve exclaimed. "You think *every* day is the perfect day for finding a ghost! And you haven't found one yet. When are you going to admit that they don't exist?"

"When are you going to admit that they *do?*" I asked. "There are lots of ghosts on Fear Street. Just because you haven't seen one yet doesn't mean they're not there."

I could tell Steve wanted to interrupt me. I took a deep breath and rushed on. "Remember what Zack Pepper told me? His substitute teacher was really a ghost—and she almost pulled him back into her grave! Do you think that Zack is a liar?"

Steve shook his head. "No. Not a liar," he said. "Just crazy like you."

"Well, I believe him," I said. "Every single word."

My brother laughed. "That's the trouble with you, Dylan, my lad. You believe everything you hear. When you're my age, you'll know better."

I hate it when Steve calls me "my lad." I hate it more than I hate being tickled.

And I hate it when he says, "when you're my age." Steve's only one year older than I am. *One* year. He's in the sixth grade. I'm in the fifth. And he doesn't look older than me either. In fact, some people confuse us—we look that much alike. We both have blond hair, big green eyes, and tons of freckles.

"Whatever you say, Grandpa," I shot back.

Steve smiled one of his I'm-so-much-more-

5

mature-than-you smiles and said, "Well, at least I'm old enough to know that there's no such thing as . . ."

Steve didn't finish his sentence.

He caught sight of something out the window. And now his eyes were locked on it.

He gasped.

"What?" I cried. "What is it?"

Steve swallowed hard. I could see the muscles in his neck pop out. "A-a ghost," he whispered, pointing outside with a shaky finger.

"Where?" I yelled.

I forgot I was angry and leaped forward so fast I smashed my face into the window. My nose felt as if someone had punched me. Hard.

But I didn't care. I shoved Steve aside so I could look for the ghost.

Then I heard a horrible sound.

A truly horrible sound.

Steve. Laughing.

"It's—it's—Pokey the dog," he stuttered. "The most hideous pooch to haunt Fear Street. I guess I made a little mistake," Steve said with a mean laugh.

I flopped down into the green chair and grabbed my book. "Someday I'm going to see a real ghost," I informed Steve. "And when I do, I won't even bother telling you about it."

6

"I'm really hurt," Steve wailed in a high little voice. Then he gave a loud sniffle.

I opened the book and pretended to read. Maybe Steve would take the hint and leave. He didn't.

"You would never see a ghost even if they did exist—which they don't," he continued. "Nothing exciting ever happens to *you.* And, if by some miracle you did see a ghost, you'd probably turn around and—"

BOOOOOM!

A thundering crash split the air.

The whole house rocked.

The lamp next to my chair toppled over and the lightbulb shattered, plunging us into darkness.

"St-Steve," I croaked. "Wh-what was that?"

2

"**I**t-it came from the backyard," Steve whispered. His voice trembled slightly.

"Let's go see."

We tore through the house and out the back door. I jumped down the steps and almost landed right on top of my dad.

"Hi, guys," Dad called. "Guess you heard the crash." He put down the chain saw he was carrying.

"Crash? What crash?" Steve said, back to sounding like his usual obnoxious self.

"We heard it, Dad. What happened?" I asked.

Dad waved his hand toward the right side of the yard. A huge tree lay stretched out on the grass. It covered almost half our lawn.

"It's time to start clearing out the trees, boys," he explained, "if we want to get our pool in before summer."

"It looks like you almost cleared out the house, Dad," Steve joked.

For once I agreed with Steve. The top branches of the tree brushed against the house. If the tree had been a little bit taller, it would have slammed through the roof.

Dad wiped a bead of sweat from his face with a rag and laughed so hard his whole body shook up and down.

"Ha-ha. That's a good one, Steve. Ha-ho-ho!"

I rolled my eyes in disgust. My father always acts like Steve is a laugh riot. He never even understands my jokes.

Dad and Steve looked at the fallen tree as if they were scientists studying a moon rock.

"I guess I must have figured out the angle wrong on that one somehow," Dad said.

Steve shook his head as if he really had an opinion about the correct angle. Sometimes my brother just makes me sick.

I wandered over to the gap in the woods left by the huge tree. I could see into a part of the Fear Street woods I'd never been in. And way in the distance I saw something amazing.

"Steve," I yelled. "Steve, you are absolutely not

9

going to believe what's out there." Steve didn't look up.

"Steve!" I hollered. "Come on! Look! I think I see a tree house."

"Where?" Steve actually sounded a little interested.

"There, way deep in the woods. You can just see the top of it." I pointed straight ahead into the deep woods.

"Oh, yeah, I see what you mean," Steve admitted. "It might be a tree house—but how come we never saw it before?"

"I don't know, the branches of the other trees must have hidden it. Come on, let's go look for it."

Steve yawned. "I think I'll go inside and watch some TV," he said. "Tell me if you find it."

Is my brother the laziest person in the world, or what? "No way!" I answered. "I'm going to find the tree house. And I'm claiming it for myself!"

"Okay, okay," Steve said quickly. "I'll come with you. Just to make sure you don't get lost."

I knew that would get him. Steve can't stand it if I have something he doesn't.

"Don't go too far, guys," Dad warned. "It's almost dinnertime. I'm making my rigatoni with spicy meatballs tonight. It has to be served as soon as it's ready, or else it tastes like glue."

10

"Sure, Dad," I answered. Then I plunged into the woods and trotted along the rocky, overgrown trail.

Steve followed behind me. Complaining. As usual. "This path is bumpy," he griped. "And it's freezing out here!"

"You're right," I admitted. "I wonder why it's so cold."

I noticed my breath making frosty little clouds in front of my face. It *is* chilly for April, I thought. And the air seems to be getting colder with every step we take.

Steve tripped over a rock and fell flat on his face. He flipped over and glared at the rip in the knee of his favorite jeans. "This path stinks!" he yelled. "I'm going back."

I grabbed his arm and hauled him to his feet. "Let's keep going for a little while longer," I begged.

I didn't understand it, but something seemed to be pulling me into the woods. I couldn't stop now.

"No! I'm out of here." Steve turned and started back to the house.

"Wait! I have a deal for you."

Steve spun around. He loves deals. "It better be good," he warned.

"I'll do your paper route tomorrow morning."

He shook his head. "Not good enough," he said. "But if you deliver my papers every morning it rains from now until the end of the year, I'll stay out here five more minutes. That's it. Take it or leave it."

"Ten more minutes," I said.

Steve nodded. "It's a deal."

We followed the overgrown path around a sharp curve—and that's when I saw it.

I stopped short and Steve bashed into me.

"What's wrong with you?" he complained.

I didn't speak. I couldn't.

I pointed to the top of a huge black oak tree standing alone in a clearing. On one side of the tree, an enormous branch rose up like a huge twisted arm, reaching up into the dark sky. Between the branch and the trunk, I could just see the remains of a platform, and a jagged section of wall.

The tree house.

"It looks like somebody dropped a bomb on it or something," Steve observed.

I trotted halfway across the clearing. "Look there," I whispered, pointing to the trunk of the black oak. "It used to have two levels. See that ladder that starts near the ground? It leads to a platform below the other one."

I noticed that half of the bottom platform was charred black. And there were no branches on that side of the tree.

I closed my eyes for a second and tried to picture

12

the tree house with both levels rebuilt. "This is so cool," I whispered.

"Great. Come on. Your ten minutes are up," Steve said.

I walked to the oak. Then I stopped.

I froze in horror.

Someone—or something—was standing at the base of the tree.

Almost hidden in the shadows.

It was a dark, shadowy, formless *thing* and I could see its eyes. Its cold, dark eyes.

And they were staring straight at me.

3

I opened my mouth to call my brother's name. But no sounds came out. My lips were suddenly too stiff to form words.

I silently told my legs to walk forward, toward the shapeless *thing*.

I was terrified, but I had to know whether it was a ghost. I had to find out if it even existed, or whether I was just imagining it.

But I just couldn't make myself move!

I swallowed hard three times. At last I was able to croak out a few words. "Steve," I whispered, "do you see that?"

"What?" Steve's voice rang out in the woods.

"What did you say, Dylan? Why are you whispering like that? I can't hear a word you're saying."

His words sounded so loud in the eerie silence. "Don't you see that . . . that *thing* over there by the tree?" I asked again. But before I'd even finished my sentence, the black form melted away into the shadows.

"Give it a rest, Dylan," Steve said.

"But I saw it!" I insisted, squinting at the tree. "A big, black kind of blobby shape. It was looking right at me, and . . ."

"Dy-lan! Steve! Din-ner!" My father's booming voice carried through the cold, clammy air. But he sounded so far away. "On the doub-le!"

"Come on." Steve yanked my arm.

But I was frozen to the spot. Staring at the tree. Hoping I'd see the shadowy figure one more time.

"You stay here if you want," Steve muttered. "I'm going home to eat."

"Okay, okay," I mumbled. "But can we come back?"

"Yeah, sure. We can come back," Steve said. "Another time. Like maybe in a hundred years."

Steve started back on the bumpy path. I glanced at the tree house one last time. Everything remained still.

That's when I realized how totally quiet the woods were.

15

No sounds at all.

Not even the chirp of a single bird.

Weird. Definitely weird.

I slowly turned and followed my brother. *I'm coming back,* I promised myself. *No matter how creepy these woods are . . . I'm coming back. This could finally be my chance to meet a ghost!*

As we hurried home, I noticed something else about the woods that was strange. The farther we got from the tree house, the warmer I felt.

Didn't one of my ghost books talk about cold spots in haunted houses? I had to read up on all the signs of ghost appearances right away!

Steve led the way inside, telling Mom and Dad, "Dylan's seeing things again." He really does treat me like a baby.

In the bright light of the kitchen I could hardly believe I'd seen the shadowy ghost out in the woods. But I knew I had. And I couldn't stop thinking about it.

During dinner I dribbled Dad's tomato sauce down my shirt. And Mom had to ask me three times to pass the bread.

I could hear Steve snickering at me, but I didn't care. The second I was excused from the table, I ran upstairs to my bedroom. I had to start my ghost research.

Steve barged into the room a few minutes later

and dropped down on the bottom bunk of our bunk beds. Then he reached into his backpack, pulled out a book, and groaned.

I already knew what was coming.

"Dylan, my lad, I have—"

"A deal for you," I finished.

"This is a really good one," Steve protested. "You write my social studies report for me, and I'll take back any rainy Mondays, Wednesdays, and Fridays for delivering my newspapers."

I noticed this deal left me with four days a week, while Steve had three.

And he stuck me with the Sunday papers.

Everyone knows those are the heaviest.

"No deal. I'll take my chances with the rain." I reached over to my bookshelf, grabbed my copy of *The A–Z Ghost Encyclopedia,* and looked up cold spots.

The encyclopedia confirmed that cold was a sign of a haunted place.

I knew it!

"What then?" Steve asked. He still hadn't bothered to open his social studies book. "What kind of deal do you want to make?"

"How about I write the paper, and you help me rebuild the tree house?" I suggested. "That—or nothing," I quickly added. I've learned a few things from Steve.

17

"No *way* am I helping you rebuild that tree house," Steve answered. "That would take as long as writing a hundred papers. That place is a total wreck."

"But think how cool it could be." I sat down at my desk, grabbed a big sheet of paper, and started sketching. "A two-level tree house of our own—where no one would bother us."

"It wouldn't be worth the work," Steve mumbled.

I ignored him and kept drawing. Then I held up the sketch.

"Whoa!" Steve exclaimed. "Do you really think you could make that awesome pulley thing and rebuild the second floor?"

"Sure. But I would definitely need your help on it."

That wasn't quite true. Steve would probably drive me nuts the whole time. But if the shadowy thing really *was* a ghost—and if it came back—I wanted Steve to see it. So I could prove to him—finally—that ghosts were real!

"Come on, Steve," I continued. "It'll be a cool place to hang out. And nobody could bug us about doing our homework up there." I left my chair and glanced out the window to see if I could spot the tree house.

"Hmmmm," Steve thought a minute, brushing

18

his hair back under his baseball cap. "Okay, I'm in."

Do I know the right thing to say to my brother, or what?

"But you have to do more of the work," Steve added. "Because you're the one who really wants the tree house."

"You are so . . ." My voice trailed off.

"So what?" Steve asked.

I didn't answer him.

I was staring out the window. Right where I thought the tree house stood.

"Look!" I shouted. "Look! There! A light—out by the tree house."

"You're probably seeing things, as usual," Steve grumbled. He rolled off the bed and shuffled over to the window. He leaned close to the glass and cupped his hands around his eyes. "Hey! There *is* a light bouncing around out there."

"Why would someone be out in the woods at night?" I wondered out loud.

"That's a good question," Steve replied.

We stared out the window in silence. Watching the light bob and flicker.

Could it be the ghost? Maybe, I decided. But why would a ghost need light?

There was only one way to find out for sure. "Let's go and check it out," I said quietly.

To my amazement, Steve didn't argue or try to make a deal. He pulled a sweatshirt out of his middle drawer and yanked it over his head.

"This time, I'm not going to freeze to death," he announced. "Come on. What are you waiting for?" Steve grinned at me and slapped me a high five.

Every once in a while having a brother can be cool.

Steve turned on the radio before we left our room. "Better have some noise in here."

Steve was right—sometimes Mom and Dad get suspicious if we are *too* quiet. Dad claims it's because they're afraid we've killed each other. Ha-ha.

I followed Steve down the stairs. We both stepped over the third step. That's the one that creaks.

As we crept through the kitchen I snagged a flashlight from the junk drawer. We cut across the backyard and entered the woods. Then I flipped the flashlight on.

It didn't help much. We both tripped over rocks and roots. We'd only gone about three feet when Steve started asking the same question over and over again.

"Why?" he chanted. "Why, why, why? Why did I agree to do this?" With each step he took, he muttered, "Why?"

I wanted to tell him to shut up. But I didn't want to make him angry. I didn't want him to turn back.

When we had made it about halfway there, Steve changed his chant. He changed it to "Cold. Cold, cold, cold."

He was really getting annoying now. But I had to admit it—it was cold. I was shivering.

But that was a good sign!

Yes. Cold was definitely a good sign.

Because cold meant ghosts!

"Do you see anything?" Steve whispered in my ear.

"No—wait. Maybe." I stared hard at the big oak tree. "There!" I pointed. "I just saw a light on that side of the tree. Then it went out."

I dug my heels into the ground—planting them there firmly—so it would be harder to bolt, which is exactly what I wanted to do.

I cleared my throat.

"Who is there?" My voice squeaked.

The light flashed again.

Then it went out.

Swoosh, swoosh, swoosh.

"D-did you hear that?" I asked Steve. He nodded.

Something was moving in the dark.

Swoosh, swoosh, swoosh.

21

There it was again. Like ghostly feet sliding over the grass. Moving. Toward us.

I swung the flashlight around wildly. Trying to catch it in my beam.

Then I heard another sound. A voice. A laugh.

"Steve, did you hear that?" I whispered. "It laughed."

"Shine your light over there," Steve whispered back.

He sounded scared. I knew I was.

I swung my flashlight in that direction—and two humanlike forms walked toward us.

Girls.

Two girls squinting in the light and giggling.

Two totally alive girls.

4

I wanted a ghost. Or a werewolf. Or a vampire. Even a mummy.

But no. I found girls.

"Who are you?" Steve asked as we walked toward them. "What are you doing out here?"

"I'm Kate Drennan," one of the girls answered in a soft voice. "And this is my sister, Betsy."

Both girls had bright blue eyes and long black hair. The one named Kate had straight hair tied back in a ponytail. The other one had wavy hair with curls that tumbled all the way down her back.

I'd never seen either of them before—even though they looked as though they should be in my grade.

"We were just—" Kate began again. But before she could finish, Betsy cut her off.

"Why do you get to ask the questions?" she demanded. "We have as much right to be here as you do."

"Okay, okay," I started to apologize. "It's just that I've never seen you around here before. Do you go to Shadyside Middle School?"

"No," Kate started to answer.

"We're on spring break," Betsy interrupted. "We go to school in Vermont. We don't know many kids in Shadyside, so it gets pretty boring."

"That's why we sneaked out tonight," Kate added. "We were bored. There was nothing on TV. Nothing to do."

"We sneaked out, too," I admitted.

Kate—the nicer one—smiled. And Betsy—the bossy one—seemed to relax a little.

"At least you get a vacation," Steve added. "We don't have one until school lets out for the summer."

"We should head back," Betsy said. "Our parents might check up on us or something."

"Us, too. We'll probably see you around," I volunteered. "We'll be out here a lot—we're going to rebuild that tree house."

I shone the flashlight up into the branches of the big, dark oak. Both girls glanced up. Then I noticed

24

Kate's expression. She looked scared. Really scared.

Betsy glared at me. "What did you say?" she asked.

"I said we're going to rebuild that old tree house."

"That's what I thought you said," Betsy replied. "But you can't."

"Why can't we?" Steve demanded.

"No one can," Betsy insisted.

Kate began chewing nervously on the end of her ponytail. "You can't rebuild the tree house," she said. "You can't because . . . because . . ."

"Because of the secret about it," Betsy finished for her sister.

"The secret?" I asked. "What secret?"

25

5

A tree house with a secret! Is this cool or what?

"We can't tell you. Everyone knows about this old tree house," Betsy snapped.

Then she narrowed her eyes. "But I *will* tell you this—if you don't want to get hurt . . . you'll stay away from the tree house!"

"They're just trying to scare us," Steve replied. "But it's not going to work. Right?"

"Right," I replied, not feeling as convinced as I sounded.

"Well, I, uh, really think you should listen to Betsy," Kate whispered. "Because we, um, we heard some kids tried to fix up the tree house and they . . ."

"What happened to them?" These girls were driving me crazy. "Did they die? What happened?"

Betsy shook her sister's shoulder, interrupting her for the millionth time. "Come on. Let's go. They don't need to hear that old story," she snapped. "If they're smart, they'll just stay away."

"Why? Why should we stay away?" I asked. Then I remembered what I had read about ghosts and cold spots. "Wow!" I said. "Is the tree house haunted?"

"Come on, Kate," Betsy ordered. "These guys are hopeless."

Kate gave a sort of half smile. "We do have to go," she said. "Our mom will freak if she can't find us."

"Wait!" I protested. "Just tell us some more about the tree house. Please!"

I thought Kate was about to say something, but Betsy didn't give her a chance. "I said come *on*," she grumbled, tugging her sister across the clearing.

"Bye," Kate called over her shoulder.

As they stepped onto the path, Betsy stopped and called back, "Remember, you have been warned. Now if anything bad happens to you, it will be your own fault!"

The next day at school, I couldn't concentrate. Betsy's warning kept echoing in my head. What did it mean? What was the big secret about the tree house?

It must be haunted, I decided. That had to be it. At least I hoped so.

I spent the last part of the day—the part when we were supposed to be doing math—drawing tree house plans on the cover of my notebook.

In some of the plans, I sketched a shadowy figure sitting on the end of a branch. I made it shadowy because I didn't know what a ghost really looked like. Not yet, anyway.

As soon as the last bell rang, I raced home. I headed straight into the garage and loaded up two big cardboard boxes with nails, old boards, and lots of tools.

That was the easy part.

Next came the hard part—Steve. I found him lying on the couch, watching TV, and munching Cheese Curlies.

"Come on," I said. "We have to start before it gets too dark out there."

Steve's eyes remained glued to the screen. "Let's wait till Saturday," he answered. "I want to watch the rest of this show."

I glanced at the TV. "You've seen that cartoon at least one hundred times!" I snatched the remote from his hand and clicked off the TV. "We had a deal."

"Our deal didn't say *when* I had to help," Steve answered. "What's the big rush, anyway?"

"I think the tree house is haunted! I think someone died up there! And I did see something in the shadows."

"Dylan," Steve said, shaking his head, "the only thing that died is your brain."

"I can *prove* to you that ghosts are real," I replied. "Just think about it—this is the perfect chance for us to settle our argument about ghosts. If the tree house is haunted, I know I can prove it."

Steve shoved himself up from the sofa.

"All right, Dylan, my lad. But if we don't see a ghost before we finish the tree house, you have to admit I was right and you were wrong."

"Sure. Let's go."

"*And* you have to stop talking about ghosts, reading about ghosts, watching movies about ghosts—even thinking about ghosts. Deal?" Steve asked.

"Deal," I agreed.

We headed to the garage to pick up the supplies. Steve chose the lightest box, of course.

We cut across the backyard, and I led the way into the woods. "Wow!" Steve cried as he stumbled along behind me. "The woods are even colder than last night. From now on, I'm wearing my winter parka when we come out here."

29

"It's because of the ghost," I informed him. "Haunted places usually have a colder temperature."

"Give me a break!" Steve shouted. "It's cold because of all the trees. The sunlight can't get through the branches."

After that we trudged along without talking. My box felt heavier with every step. I thought about turning around and asking Steve to trade. But I didn't want to start another argument.

I stopped when the path reached the clearing.

I scanned the shadows around the oak tree.

Nothing there.

I dumped my cardboard box on the ground. I turned to Steve—and couldn't believe what I saw. "Where's yours?" I demanded.

"Where's my what?" Steve asked, smiling.

"Your *box.*"

Steve took off his baseball cap, smoothed his hair, and stuck the cap back on. "I left it at the edge of the backyard. We couldn't possibly use all that junk in one day," Steve explained.

"That was not our deal!" I yelled. "Our deal was that you help. Watching me carry a box does not count as help. And neither does leaving our stuff behind!"

"Okay, okay. I'll get the box," Steve muttered.

I watched Steve disappear down the path—and

realized what a big mistake I had made. I'd be lucky if Steve returned—with or without the box.

In fact, I knew exactly what Steve would do. He would decide he needed a glass of water. No, a glass of water and some more Cheese Curlies—to build up his strength. And since he couldn't eat and carry the box at the same time, he'd watch a few cartoons until he finished the Curlies. And by then, it would be time for me to go home.

Well, I didn't need Steve, anyway. I really didn't expect him to do much work. I just wanted him along because the woods were kind of creepy. Which is exactly what I started thinking as I opened the carton.

It was quiet here. Way too quiet.

And dark. Steve was right about the branches. They blocked out all the sunlight.

I glanced up at the tree house and felt a shiver race up and down my spine. *You wanted to see a ghost,* I told myself. *And now's your chance.*

I forced myself to march over to the tree. I tested the first rung of the ladder nailed onto the trunk. A little wobbly, but okay, I decided.

I stepped on the rung. It held me—no problem. I tugged on the second rung before I climbed up—it felt okay, too. Only three more rungs to go.

I stared up at the tree house again. An icy breeze swept over me and my knees began to shake.

Take a deep breath, I told myself. *Don't wimp out now.*

I stepped up to the next rung.

And that's when I heard the sound.

A sickening *crack.*

My feet flew out from under me as the third rung snapped off the trunk.

I flung my arms around the tree. I kicked my legs wildly, searching for a foothold. I tried to pull myself up to the fourth rung.

My heart pounded in my chest until my feet found it. Then I clung there for a few minutes. Hugging the tree trunk tightly, trying to catch my breath.

A cold gust of wind blew. My teeth began to chatter.

I inhaled deeply. "Okay, just one more rung to go," I said out loud. But I couldn't move. I remained frozen to the spot.

Then I pictured myself talking to Steve after I'd proven that ghosts exist. "Steve, my lad," I would say, "don't feel stupid. Even though you are a year older, no one expects you to be right about everything."

That gave me the courage to go on.

I made my way to the top rung. I peered underneath the tree house and studied the platform. Half of it was badly damaged. The boards were charred black. But the other half appeared solid enough. I banged on the boards with my fist a few times just to make sure.

Then I pulled myself through the open trapdoor—and felt something touch my face. Something soft. Something airy. Something light.

I screamed.

I found the ghost!

6

I leaped back. But the ghost wrapped itself around me. It covered my face. I couldn't breathe.

"Get away from me! Get away from me!" I screamed. My arms flailed as I tried to fight it off.

Its touch was sticky. It felt like—spiderwebs.

Spiderwebs.

I wasn't battling a ghost. I was fighting spiderwebs.

I guess that should have made me feel better, but it didn't. Because the more I fought, the more tangled up I got.

I shook my hands, but the webs wouldn't come off. And my fingers started to burn and itch.

I tried to brush the webs out of my face. I could

feel them clinging to my eyelashes. They were in my ears. My nostrils. My mouth.

"Get off! Get off!" I screamed as I clawed at my face.

They pressed in tighter.

They were suffocating me.

I couldn't breathe.

I stumbled around the tree house until I found the trapdoor. Then I lowered myself through the hole. I didn't bother feeling around for the rungs. I slid all the way down the tree trunk.

When I reached the ground, Steve was standing there. "Help me get these things off!" I yelled. "They're all over me. I almost choked to death!"

Steve pulled off his jacket and brushed the webs off with it. I grabbed it and wiped my face.

"Are you okay?" Steve asked.

I nodded.

"Then give me back my jacket."

I threw it at him. He shook it out and pulled it over his head.

Even though the webs were gone, I couldn't stop scratching.

"There weren't *that* many," Steve commented as he watched me.

"I couldn't breathe!" I protested.

"You just scared yourself," he said. "You're so

convinced there's a ghost up there that you freaked."

"I almost died!" What did Steve know? He wasn't the one in the tree house.

"Hey! Maybe that's what that weird girl meant when she said the tree house was dangerous," Steve said.

"What? What do you mean?"

"Killer cobwebs," he replied.

"That's funny, Steve. Real funny." I closed up the carton with our tools and shoved it up against the tree. "We'll leave it here until tomorrow—"

When you go up to the tree house first, I added to myself. *And you're the one smothered in itchy, burning spiderwebs. Then we'll see how you like it, Steve. Then we'll see.*

The next morning was Saturday. Finally! A whole day to work on the tree house. I got up early and waited for Steve on the porch. I checked my watch. Seven A.M. Steve would be here any minute.

The minute I sat down on the front steps, Steve rounded the corner on his bicycle. He rode up and dumped his bike on the lawn.

"Ready?" I asked him, jumping up.

"Yep. Ready," he replied. He plowed past me and headed for the door. "Ready to go back to bed."

"Hey!" I cried, running to the door and bracing

both arms against the frame to block his way. "You agreed to work all day on the tree house."

"I'm going back to sleep. I'll help you when I get up." He shoved me aside.

"Doughnuts," I said just as he turned the knob. "Double-dipped chocolate doughnuts."

"You've got doughnuts?" Steve asked.

"In my backpack. Mom drove me down to the Donut Hole."

"Hand them over," Steve ordered. "Mom didn't buy them just for you." He took a few steps toward me. Then he lunged for my backpack.

"Mom didn't buy them," I said, leaping back. "*I* did. With my own money. And I'm taking them out to the tree house."

I pushed past Steve and ran around the house. I could hear his feet pounding right behind me.

Halfway to the clearing, Steve caught up to me and yanked my backpack off. He pawed through it and grabbed a doughnut with each hand.

"You'll never be able to outrun me, Dylan, my lad," Steve declared. He took a big bite of one doughnut. Then he followed me down the path.

Do I know my brother, or what?

When we reached the clearing, I handed Steve another doughnut and took one for myself. "It's your turn to deal with the spiderwebs today," I announced.

37

I pulled an old house painter's mask out of my backpack and tossed it to Steve. "Wear this. At least it will keep the webs out of your nose and mouth."

"I don't need it," he said, tossing it aside. Then he began climbing up the tree.

I stared up and watched him climb. Even though it was a bright sunny morning, the tree house was cloaked in darkness. A breeze rustled the leaves. A cold breeze.

Steve entered the tree house through the trap-door. "Oh, no!" he cried out.

"What?" I yelled. "Is it the ghost?"

"No, you idiot. I forgot to take the hammer," he replied, laughing. "Hand it up to me. The one with the big claw on the end. I'll need to pry some of these boards up. And give me some new boards, too, while you're at it."

No ghosts. No spiderwebs.

I wasn't sure what disappointed me more. I handed Steve the stuff he needed. Then I started working on a new ladder. I grabbed a saw from one of the cardboard boxes and found some small pieces of wood that I could cut into rungs.

As I sawed, I kept thinking about the spiderwebs. Maybe Steve was right. Maybe I just panicked yesterday.

But maybe, I thought, *just maybe, the ghost*

wrapped all those webs around my head. One of my books said some ghosts would do anything to keep humans away.

I yanked off the old rungs and began hammering the new ones into place. I was rummaging through the carton to find some nails when I realized I didn't hear Steve hammering anymore.

"Steve? How's it going up there?" I called.

No answer.

He better not be sleeping, I thought. *Not after I spent my allowance on his favorite doughnuts.*

"Steve?"

No reply.

"I'd better wake him up," I said, grumbling. I climbed up the first two rungs of the ladder and peered up.

And that's when I saw it.

The hammer.

With the big black claw at one end.

Plunging down.

Plunging straight for my face.

7

I let go of the tree and hurled myself to the ground.

Thwack! The hammer landed inches away from my nose.

"Steve!" I yelled. "You almost killed me with that hammer."

I shoved myself to my feet. My jeans were torn and my knee throbbed.

"Don't pretend you aren't up there," I bellowed.

Still no answer.

I scrambled up the rungs and poked my head through the trapdoor. No Steve.

"Now what are you screaming about, Dylan, my lad?" Steve stood halfway across the clearing, holding a bag of Cheese Curlies.

"How—how did you get over there?"

"I went back to the house for these," he said, holding up the orange bag. "You were so busy sawing you didn't notice." He grinned. "Want some?"

"No, I don't want some," I shouted. "Your hammer almost hit me in the head. Why did you leave it near the trapdoor?" I asked.

"I didn't," Steve replied. "I left it in the middle of the platform."

"You did not," I screamed.

"Did, too," Steve screamed back.

"Hey, is something wrong?" It was that girl Betsy. She and her sister, Kate, stepped out from behind the tree.

"We heard yelling," Kate said. "We thought someone was hurt." She tugged on the end of her ponytail.

"Someone *was* almost hurt." I glared at Steve. "Me. That thing came flying straight at me," I said, pointing to the hammer on the ground. "It could have smashed my head open."

"What thing?" Kate asked. Her eyes showed real concern—fear, even.

"Steve's hammer. He left it on the edge and it fell and nearly killed me." I was practically shouting.

"That's just what happened the last time," Betsy said.

Then they both nodded.

"What happened? What last time?" Now Steve was shouting.

"You must have made it very angry," Betsy said.

"I made the hammer angry? Are you crazy?" I was practically yelling at them. Why did they always have to talk in riddles?

"Not the hammer," Kate whispered. *"It."*

"Who is *it?*" I demanded.

"There is no *it*," Steve cut in. "Get real, Dylan. The wind probably blew the hammer down. Or a squirrel knocked it over."

"Believe whatever you want." Betsy smirked. "But we warned you. We warned you not to work on the tree house."

I turned toward Kate. She was chewing the end of her ponytail now.

"You made it angry," Betsy said again. "It's not a good idea to make a ghost angry."

8

"**T**ell me. Tell me about the ghost," I begged.

"I guess we have to tell them." Betsy turned toward her sister. "If we don't, they'll never finish the tree house—alive."

The four of us sat down in a circle. Betsy's eyes darted around the clearing. "I don't know if it's safe to tell this—especially so close to where it happened."

"Please—" I started.

Betsy held up her hand, signaling me to shut up. Then she began the story.

"A long time ago three kids around our age built the tree house. They drew hundreds of pictures of it first—until they agreed on how it should look.

They wanted it to be the most perfect tree house ever. Then they spent weeks and weeks up there. Hammering. Sawing. Making sure everything fit just right."

"Ooooh, I'm starting to get scared already," Steve said, rolling his eyes.

"Ignore him," I told Betsy.

"The night the tree house was finished, the kids decided to sleep in it. They brought some food and their sleeping bags. And they stayed up late— telling ghost stories.

"Suddenly, a thunderstorm rolled in. Streaks of lightning cut through the sky. But the kids weren't scared. They thought it was cool to be there. A great night for ghost stories."

I nodded. I know how much I like to read my ghost books when it's cold and gray. Ghost weather.

"Then a strong wind picked up. The branches beneath the tree house began to sway. And the tree house creaked and groaned. A blast of thunder made the tree shake. They all screamed in terror.

"They talked about going home. But the rain was coming down hard now. They decided to wait out the storm. Strong storms like these never lasted long, they thought.

"And then it happened.

"A lightning bolt shattered the clouds. It sliced

44

through the heavy treetops and pierced the tree house.

"The tree house burst into flames."

Betsy swallowed hard.

Lightning. That made sense. I remembered the charred black boards in the lower platform.

"The kids were up on the top platform," Betsy continued. "They couldn't escape. The horrible flames leaped up in front of them. Behind them.

"Thick black smoke billowed everywhere.

"They cried out for help—but it was too late."

"Some people say you can still hear their terrifying screams on rainy nights," Kate whispered.

I stared over at the tree house. I pictured it in flames. I imagined the cries. The horrible cries for help. I shuddered.

"So that's it?" Steve asked. "That's why we shouldn't build the tree house? We're not dumb enough to stay in a tree house in a thunderstorm."

"That's not why," I said. I understood what Betsy was trying to tell us. "The tree house is haunted now, right? It's haunted by the ghosts of the kids."

Betsy nodded. Then she went on.

"Many years after the accident, some kids tried to rebuild the tree house. But they didn't have time to finish it. . . ."

45

"What happened to them?" I whispered. I could feel my heart pounding in my chest as Betsy continued.

"No one knows the whole story. At first, little things went wrong. One of the boys fell off the ladder—a rung broke."

"Big deal," Steve interrupted. "The wood was probably old—so it broke."

Betsy continued. "But it wasn't an old rung—it was one of the new ones they had just fixed. Another kid came down with a strange fever. It turned out he had like a million spider bites."

Spider bites.

I could feel the spiderwebs on my face as she talked.

"Then things got really strange. No matter how hard they worked—the tree house was never finished. Boards that were hammered in one day were found on the ground the next day.

"Finally the kids realized the tree house was haunted. They stopped working on it—all except for one kid. I think his name was Duncan."

"What happened to Duncan?" Steve asked.

"He kept working on the tree house. Until . . . until one day his brother found him. He was lying under the tree house. A hammer had fallen and knocked him out."

"Was he dead?" I managed to croak.

"No one knows," Kate said. "His family moved away after that. And no one has dared to go near the tree house since then."

I glanced around the woods. Nothing moved. Everything was silent. So silent I could hear Kate's soft breathing across from me.

"Now you know why you can't work on the tree house," Kate said. "We probably shouldn't even be in this clearing. We're too close. Much too close."

"You're right," Betsy said. "Let's get out of here. This place is giving me the creeps."

"Are you going?" Kate asked.

I didn't answer. There were too many thoughts racing around in my brain. The webs . . . The hammer . . . That kid Duncan . . . The haunted tree house . . .

"We've got some stuff to do," I finally answered. "We'll see you around."

Betsy gave me a long, hard stare. "I don't think you're going to be around much longer," she said. "Not if you stay here."

Then she grabbed Kate's arm and they ran across the clearing and disappeared into the woods.

"Those girls are seriously weird," Steve said. "Even weirder than you, Dylan. They're really scared some ghost is going to swoop down and grab them."

"You don't think that story is true?" I asked.

"Of course not," Steve shot back. "Ghosts don't exist, Dylan, my lad. Trust me. I'm older. I know more than you do."

Yeah, right, I thought. "Then how did that story get started? And what happened to the hammer in the middle of the platform? How come it fell on me?"

Steve groaned.

"I'll tell you how come that hammer fell," I said to Steve. "The ghost threw it at me—as a warning!"

9

I managed to trick, bargain, or bribe Steve into working on the tree house every day until Friday. On Fridays Steve has band practice. He smashes cymbals together once or twice during a concert— then he brags about what a great musician he is.

So I had to go out to the tree house alone. *This probably isn't such a good idea,* I thought as I walked through the woods. The ghost Kate and Betsy had described didn't exactly sound friendly. But if there was a ghost out there, I wanted to see it, I decided. No matter what.

I thought about the girls' story—the broken rung on the ladder. The spider bites. The hammer.

The hammer. A shiver ran through me. I sure

was luckier than that boy Duncan. But would my luck hold out?

The clearing was just up ahead.

I walked a few steps into it and stopped.

"Oh, no!" I groaned.

All our boards and nails—all of them—had been destroyed.

They lay scattered everywhere—all over the clearing, between the trees—everywhere. I even spotted some boards on the ground deep in the forest.

They were all bent and twisted. Deformed.

I swallowed hard and stared up at the dark windows of the tree house. Nothing moved inside.

I slowly crossed the clearing.

I glanced up at the tree house before each step.

I was terrified—terrified that the ghost was getting ready to swoop down on me.

I reached the base of the old oak and stood there. Waiting. Waiting for something to happen.

Nothing did.

So I began cleaning up the mess, nervously checking over my shoulder every few minutes.

It would take me hours to find all the nails and clean up this mess. Now I was more angry than scared.

"It's going to take more than this to stop me!" I yelled out. "I'm not like those other kids!"

When I stopped screaming the woods felt quieter than ever. Spookier.

That's right, Dylan, I thought. *Invite the ghost to come out and pound you. Very smart.*

I glanced around. Nothing moved.

I grabbed one of the cardboard boxes and began tossing nails into it. Nails that I had straightened out. This was going to take forever.

At this moment the only one I hated more than the ghost was Steve. How come he always manages to be busy when I need him the most?

After I had gathered up all the nails I could find, I began collecting the boards. I stacked up the ones in the clearing first. Then I gathered the others that had been tossed in the woods.

As I hauled the last one back to the clearing, I peered up at the tree house—and spotted something high on the trunk.

I wasn't sure what it was. I walked a few steps closer and squinted.

Claw marks.

It looked like claw marks.

Huge, black claw marks.

I'd never seen an animal with claws big enough to make those marks. And I wasn't even sure a big animal could get way up there.

But there was one thing I *was* sure about—those marks weren't there yesterday.

51

I moved closer to the tree and stared hard. That's when I realized I wasn't staring at claw marks.

I was looking at something worse. Much worse.

They were letters. Letters burned into the trunk of the tree.

My heart pounded as I spelled out the message. S-T-A-Y-A-W-A-Y.

Stay away!

10

~~~~~~

"**G**et real, Dylan," Steve said. "For the hundredth time, there are no ghosts. Not here. Not in the tree house. Not anywhere."

"What about the letters?" I spat back.

"Well, Dylan, my lad. I have a theory about those letters. I think you put them there," he said, "to make me believe in ghosts. It was a nice try—but it's not going to work."

I wanted to strangle Steve.

But I made a suggestion instead.

"We can settle our ghost argument once and for all tonight," I told him.

"Why? What happens tonight?" he asked.

"Tonight we are going to sleep out in the woods. And we are going to finally meet a ghost."

It took the usual arguments before Steve agreed to sleep outside with me that night.

"You want me to camp out in the freezing cold— without any TV? Are you crazy?" he hollered.

"You're not afraid, are you?" I challenged.

"How can I be afraid of something that doesn't exist?" Steve snapped. "You're the one who's always getting spooked. I'm just not doing it—that's all."

"Do you still have that book report to write for your English class?" I asked.

And that was the end of that. Steve and I were going to sleep out.

"The deal was that I sleep out with you tonight," Steve said as he squirmed his way into his sleeping bag. "That means I sleep. You watch."

"How am I going to prove ghosts exist if I can't wake you up when one appears?" I argued.

"It's not going to happen, Dylan," he answered. He closed his eyes and rolled over on his side. "But if it does, if by some miracle you're right and I'm wrong and you find a ghost—you can wake me up. But you'd better be absolutely sure it's a ghost. Or I'll pound you."

54

My brother is such an idiot, I thought. But it's better to be out in the woods with an idiot than with no one at all.

I didn't plan to sleep. So I sat cross-legged on my sleeping bag, with my flashlight, camera, and tape recorder all ready to go.

I also had a thermometer so I'd know how cold the ghost made the air. And a compass—to study its effect on the earth's magnetic field.

I even put a plate of cookies and crackers and Cheese Curlies at the bottom of the oak tree. I'd always wondered if ghosts ate. None of my books mentioned food. But I wanted to be prepared for anything.

I was ready.

I pressed the record button on the tape recorder. "Testing one, two. Testing. This is Dylan S. Brown," I whispered into it. It is Friday, April 21st, 10:38 P.M. My assistant, Steve Brown, and I successfully sneaked out of the house.

"We have set up a base camp in the Fear Street Woods, near the clearing next to the tree house. I hope the trees will hide us from the ghost. I want to observe it before I decide to make contact. It is too dark to photograph the words I discovered burned into the tree trunk. I will document them tomorrow."

Steve gave a little half-snort, half-snore. "My assistant has fallen asleep," I continued. "More later." I clicked off the tape recorder.

I raised my binoculars and studied the tree house.

No lights.

No movement.

Nothing staring back at me.

I let the binoculars fall back around my neck.

Then I heard a rustling sound. Not very loud—but coming from the direction of the tree house.

Something was definitely out there.

I thought about waking Steve up. But I didn't. I wasn't sure yet if it was the ghost. And if it wasn't, he'd kill me.

I picked up my binoculars and pressed them to my face.

I peered into the darkness.

I couldn't see a thing.

Should I turn on my flashlight? I wanted to, but if I did whatever was out there would see me. And I didn't want to scare it off.

I listened hard. There it was again. That same rustling sound. Even though I was wearing my blue winter parka, I shivered. The air around me felt colder now.

I checked the thermometer. Five degrees cooler than before. I knew it!

My pulse began to race. Chills ran up and down my spine.

I should be taping this, I thought. With a shaky hand I punched on the record button.

Should I wake Steve up now?

No. Not yet. I needed more proof.

The noise again. Louder this time.

Part of me wanted to duck down into my sleeping bag and zip it over my head. But I couldn't. I had to get closer. I had to see my ghost.

I picked up the flashlight and crawled away from my sleeping bag. I dodged behind the closest tree. The noise continued. The ghost didn't spot me.

I stayed low to the ground—on my hands and knees.

Crawling from tree to tree.

Crawling closer to the old oak.

My heart pounded so hard I thought it would burst out of my chest.

But now I was there. Behind a large rock right next to the old oak.

I peeked out from behind my hiding spot. Too dark. I still couldn't see anything. But I could hear it.

I steadied my flashlight in my trembling hand. I held it straight out in front of me. I flipped it on.

Two cold, dark eyes were caught in its beam.

A cat.

A gray cat eating Cheese Curlies.

I let out the longest sigh of my life.

Beads of sweat dripped from my forehead. I sank back against the tree and wiped them off.

Creak.

I jerked my head back toward the old oak.

Creak.

The cat darted into the woods.

Creak.

I recognized that sound—the sound of someone walking on the old wooden boards of the tree house.

Creak. Creak.

This is it, I thought. This is really it. I stood up and inched closer to the tree house.

I held my breath. I was afraid to breathe. Afraid the ghost would hear me.

I stood a foot away from the tree house. I squinted up into the darkness.

One of the boards on the wall of the tree house moved . . . as if someone up there was shaking it.

I heard the sound of nails—nails squealing as they were pried loose.

Then *pop!* I saw the board flip up. And suddenly, as I watched, it came hurtling through the air.

"Steve!" I shrieked. "Steve! It's the ghost. It's the ghost. It's tearing apart our tree house!"

CRASH!

The board hit the ground a few feet from me.

Ping ping ping.

Nails flew through the air, bouncing off the branches of the surrounding trees.

I raced over to Steve. I shook him hard. "Get up!" I screamed. "Get up!"

"What?" he muttered, rubbing his eyes.

Creak!

"Run!" I yelled. "Run! It's coming after us."

Another board came soaring out of the tree house.

THUD!

It hit the ground right next to my sleeping bag.

I tore down the path. Steve was right behind me. We had to get home before the ghost grabbed us.

I couldn't see where I was going. But I didn't slow down.

A tree branch slashed across my face. A trickle of blood dripped down my cheek. I kept running. My lungs burned. I gasped for air.

My aching legs cried out for me to stop. But I couldn't stop. Not now.

I burst into the backyard.

Did Steve make it?

I spun around to check.

He almost ran right into me. "What did you—" he began.

Then his mouth dropped open. He was staring at something over my shoulder. "Oh, no," he whispered.

Then I felt it. Something big, cold, and clammy clutching the back of my shirt.

It grabbed the back of my neck and pulled me across the wet grass!

12

My knees buckled underneath me. I began to sink to the ground.

"Let me go!" I screamed. "I promise I'll stay away from your tree house!" But the ghost raised me up.

"What are you doing out here?"

Dad.

"We were camping out to catch a ghost," I explained in a rush. "It came after us. We almost didn't get away in time."

"What's going on out there?" Mom stood under the back door light. I could see her tighten the belt on her old pink robe.

"In the house," Dad ordered us. "Dylan and

Steve were hunting ghosts in the woods," he explained to Mom.

She held the door open for us. "How could you go out this late at night?" she asked, really angry.

"Why were you running?" Dad asked. "What happened?"

"Nothing happened," Steve muttered. He sounded totally calm.

"Nothing happened?" I squeaked. "The ghost—"

"It's late," Dad interrupted. "You two get to bed. We'll discuss this in the morning."

Steve and I slunk up the stairs to our room. "What do you mean nothing happened?" I demanded the second Steve shut the door behind us.

"I mean nothing happened," Steve answered. "You got scared and ran back here. I came after you."

"Oh, right!" I cried. "You were scared, too."

"No, I wasn't," Steve replied. "There was nothing to be scared of."

"What about the board? You saw the board crash to the ground."

"Oh, that's a really big deal," Steve said, laughing. "A board from an old wrecked tree house fell down. A tree house that's falling apart. What a shock!"

"It wasn't just one board," I protested. "And it

didn't just come loose. The ghost pried it loose. It's just like what happened to the kids Betsy told us about. The ghost doesn't want us to finish the tree house—so he's taking it apart."

"Listen to me," Steve replied. "I'm older. I know more than you do. And there are no such things as ghosts, Dylan. No ghosts! No ghosts!"

"You don't know that for sure."

Steve jumped off his bed. He pulled a pair of high-tops out of the closet and pulled them on. "You are driving me insane. We're going back to the tree house. Right now."

"What?"

"You heard me." Steve pulled on a red sweatshirt over the one he already wore. "We're settling this ghost thing tonight. We're going to check out the tree house. And you're going to admit that there's no such things as ghosts."

Steve opened our door. "Come on," he whispered.

I didn't move.

I didn't need any more proof of ghosts. And I didn't care what Steve thought.

I had seen enough.

Ghosts were real.

And scary.

"Dylan! Let's go."

I shook my head no.

"Aha! So you admit it!" he cried.

Half of me wanted to jump in bed and never come out. The other half wanted to strangle Steve.

I had no choice. I crept down the stairs after my brother.

"Ssstop," Steve hissed when we were almost to the kitchen door. "Mom and Dad are in there."

We froze. "I'm worried about Dylan," Mom said. "All he talks about is ghosts. He has no other interests."

"You should have seen him in the backyard. He looked terrified. Maybe tonight was enough to convince him to give up," Dad replied.

"I hope so," Mom answered. "Why don't you go up and check on them."

"Go!" Steve whispered. He pushed me toward the stairs.

We flew up to our room. Steve eased our door shut. I scrambled into the top bunk and pulled up the covers.

I heard Dad coming up the stairs. Oh, no! We left the light on. Too late to do anything about it.

I squeezed my eyes shut and tried to breathe deeply.

Our door opened. "Must be even more scared than I thought," Dad muttered. "They left the light on."

That's when I realized my right foot was sticking out of the covers.

And I still had my shoes on. If Dad noticed my sneaker, it was over.

Dad stood in the doorway for a long moment. Should I pull my foot in? Or would that draw attention to it?

I knew I'd never be able to come up with a good excuse for going to bed with my shoes on.

Dad took a step into the room.

My eye started to twitch. A nervous twitch.

I waited . . . and heard Dad snap off the light and shut our door.

Yes!

"Let's wait about an hour for Mom and Dad to go to sleep," Steve whispered. "Then we're going back out there. Because this is the last night you'll ever say the word *ghost* again!"

An hour later I was staring up at the tree house.

"Keep going," Steve ordered. "We're checking out every inch of it." He shoved me toward the rungs.

I didn't hear any creaks. Or any squealing nails. *That's a good sign,* I told myself. The ghost probably left.

But a tiny movement in the far corner of the

second level caught my eye. Then I saw a shadowy form move down to the first floor.

I dug my fingers into Steve's arm.

"Ow!" Steve complained.

"Do you see it?" I whispered. "Look!"

Steve peered up.

His eyes were glued to the tree house.

To the ghost who was waiting there.

13

"I don't see anything," Steve declared. "Now climb up."

"The ghost is there," I insisted. "It just moved down to the bottom platform."

"Great. I can't wait to meet it," Steve said. He gave me a hard shove.

"We can't just go barging up there," I whispered. "We don't want to make it angry. Remember what happened to that boy Duncan."

Duncan. Dylan. Even our names sounded alike. I couldn't help thinking I was going to be the next ghost of Fear Street.

"Yoohoo! Mr. Ghost, we're coming to visit," Steve whispered.

He thinks he's so funny. "You go first, since you think it's all such a big joke."

"Nope. This is your ghost."

I climbed the first rung of the ladder. Steve stood right behind me.

My mouth felt totally dry. I tried to swallow, but I couldn't.

Steve poked me in the back. "Come on," he said. "It's cold here. I'm freezing."

I climbed onto the second rung. Only three more to go. *You* want *to see a ghost,* I reminded myself. *But I'd rather see it from farther away,* I added.

Steve poked me again.

I felt around for the third rung of the ladder. Then I remembered. The old board was rotten and I hadn't hammered the new one on yet.

I reached up and grabbed the fifth rung.

Then my fingers slipped. And I crashed to the ground, taking Steve with me.

I moaned as the back of my head hit a rock. I tried to lift my head, but I felt too dizzy.

I slowly opened my eyes.

And saw *two* pale faces hovering above me.

Their eyes gleamed.

Their mouths hung open wide.

Ghosts! *Two* ghosts!

Their hands stretched toward me.

Reaching. Reaching.

"Stay away!" I shrieked.

Steve saw them, too. "Run, Dylan!" he cried. "Run!"

14

Two ghosts. How could there be two ghosts?

I struggled to my feet.

"Stay away!" I shrieked.

"Don't hurt me, please," Steve cried.

"Please leave us alone!" I begged.

"Ooooooh! Ooooooh!" one of the ghosts moaned.

"Please. Please," one ghost mocked.

"Don't hurt me, please," the other one chanted.

Then they started to giggle.

They didn't cackle or howl like ghosts. They giggled like girls.

Human girls.

Betsy and Kate.

They were stretched out on their stomachs with their heads hanging out the trapdoor.

"Please leave us alone!" Betsy laughed until she choked.

And here's the worst part. Steve was laughing, too.

"Ooooh, a ghost, I'm *sooo* scared," Steve said.

I felt my face burn. My hands clenched into fists. "You think this is funny?" I demanded. "You are all sick."

Kate clambered down the ladder. Betsy followed right behind her.

"You-you're the ones who have been playing all those tricks?" I stammered. "The hammer? The boards? Everything?"

"Well, yes," Betsy admitted. "You wouldn't listen to me when I tried to tell you the tree house was haunted. So we decided to haunt it ourselves."

No ghosts. Just dumb girls teasing me. It's the story of my life. I'm never going to see a real ghost. Never.

"We really fooled you, didn't we?" Kate exclaimed. She bounced up and down, her ponytail flying.

"I know you believed every word of my ghost story," Betsy chimed in.

"No, I didn't," I protested. "I wanted to keep an

open mind. Lots of scientists believe in ghosts, and—"

"Don't lie," Steve interrupted. "Admit it. They got you good."

"We spent half the day setting up that barricade around the tree," Betsy explained. "Good thing we're on vacation. Being ghosts is hard work."

Steve started to laugh again. "I told Dylan a million times there are no such things as ghosts. But does he listen to his older—"

"Shut up!" I yelled. "All of you. Just shut up."

"Don't be angry," Kate pleaded. "We knew you wanted to see a ghost . . . and so . . . and so . . ." She ruined her apology by bursting into giggles again.

"Come on, Dylan, my lad," Steve said in that big brother voice I hate. "I'll take you home. You've had quite a scare."

"Me! What about you? You screamed when you saw them, remember?" I was so mad I could barely get the words out.

"I did not scream. Like I always say, Dylan— there are no ghosts. Now let's go home. It's way past your bedtime."

Steve and I took off across the clearing. Kate and Betsy kept calling for us to come back. But no way. I couldn't face them.

I felt like a total jerk. I couldn't speak.

72

I just headed toward home with Steve.

As soon as we were through the clearing and hidden by the woods, Steve stopped and grabbed my arm. "I'm going to kill you, Dylan. You made us look like morons."

I jerked my arm away and shoved him. "How did I make you look like a moron?" I snapped. "You laughed your head off."

"Yeah, but thanks to you I was out there sneaking around looking for *ghosts.*"

"You're always telling me how much smarter you are. Why did you bother listening to me?" I asked.

That shut him up.

We walked the rest of the way back in silence. When we reached the house, Steve opened the door and said, "You're right. I'm never listening to you again."

We stepped into the kitchen. Steve leaned close to me and whispered, "Wake up Mom and Dad and you're dead meat."

"I'm sooo scared," I whispered back.

We crept through the kitchen and up the stairs to our room. I kicked off my shoes without bothering to untie them. Mom hates that, but I was too tired to care.

I climbed straight into bed.

But I couldn't fall asleep.

I kept hearing Kate and Betsy.

Giggling.

I hate them, I thought. *I really, really hate them.*

I rolled over onto my side. Then I tried my back. Then the other side. I couldn't get comfortable.

"Stop moving around up there," Steve grumbled. "I'm trying to sleep."

"I'm trying to sleep, too." Then I rolled over and made the bed shake as much as I could.

Steve growled.

I closed my eyes. And thought.

Then I bolted up in bed.

I know what would make me feel better!

I was going to get even with Betsy and Kate.

I was going to give them the worst scare of their lives.

Now I just had to figure out how.

15

The next day started out bad. And then got worse. Steve woke me up at five A.M. because it was raining. I had to deliver his newspapers when it rained. That was the deal.

The papers weighed a ton. I couldn't throw them on a porch from the curb. So I had to get off my bike at every house and run the paper to the door. In the rain.

When I returned home, Dad handed me a list of chores that he wanted Steve and me to do. A list a mile long. They would take the rest of the day—at least.

"After you finish these," he said, "you should be

75

pretty tired. Too tired to sneak out in the middle of the night."

Ha-ha, Dad.

Before I started chore number one—clean the garage—I wanted a bowl of Froot Loops. They're my favorite cereal. But the box was empty.

I knew Steve ate the last bowl—Mom and Dad hate Froot Loops. So does Steve. But he finished them because today was get-even-with-Dylan-day—for making him look like an idiot in front of the girls.

I headed out to the garage—wet *and* hungry. I was in a really bad mood now.

I found Steve reading a comic book. Of course he hadn't started the chores without me. I asked him why.

"Why should I," he said, "when everything was your fault?"

How did I make it through the morning without killing Steve? By imagining ways to get even with Betsy and Kate. As I sorted and stacked rolls of duct tape, electrical tape, and masking tape, I pictured myself taping Kate and Betsy's mouths shut.

That way they would never be able to fool anyone again with their stupid stories.

As I organized the paint cans along one wall, I imagined dumping paint over their heads, turning their black hair green or orange. Or green *and* orange.

By the time we had cleaned the whole garage, I'd come up with about a thousand awful things to do to them.

But none of them were right.

None of them were scary enough.

In the late afternoon, after all my chores were done, I decided to visit the tree house. Just one last time, I told myself.

I wasn't afraid of meeting a ghost anymore. Not there, anyway. I still believed in ghosts—don't get me wrong. But I didn't think the tree house was haunted—except by two stupid girls.

I circled the old oak, studying the work Steve and I had done. The tree house was coming out great. The first floor was complete, and we had begun work on the second level.

I found one of the boards that Betsy and Kate had pried loose. It was lying on the grass next to one of my cardboard boxes.

I brushed the dirt off it and picked up my hammer. Then I climbed up into the tree house and hammered it back into place.

I went back down for some more boards. I had trouble getting them up into the tree by myself, but somehow I managed.

Before I knew it, it was time for dinner—and I had built two entire walls!

"I'm going to finish this tree house," I muttered. "Even if I have to do it all by myself."

The tree house will be great when it's done, I thought as I made my way back home. *And those stupid girls will be really jealous. Because I won't let them anywhere near it.*

That night I sat on my bed and stared out the window. Still plotting my revenge.

That's when I spotted the lights. Lights coming from the direction of the tree house.

"You're not going to believe this, Steve!" I exclaimed.

"I'm not listening to you," Steve informed me, without bothering to look up from his comic book.

"Oh," I said. "So you aren't interested in the fact that the girls are back out by the tree house?"

Steve jumped up and charged over to the window. "I can't believe them!" he cried. "Even you aren't dumb enough to fall for their dumb trick two nights in a row."

That's when I came up with my idea.

The perfect idea for revenge.

"No, tonight they are going to fall for one of *our* tricks," I told Steve. "Put on a black shirt, black pants, black everything."

78

"How about a black eye for you?" my very mature brother replied. "Now leave me alone."

"Please, Steve," I begged. "You have to come with me. Just one last time. To get even with those girls."

Steve glanced out the window again. I could tell he was going to change his mind.

"What's the plan?" he asked.

"Tonight *we'll* be the ghosts of the tree house," I explained. "We'll sneak up on them and scare them to death!"

Steve smiled. He grabbed his black sweatshirt and pulled it over his head. "We'll scare them good."

In a few minutes we were both dressed in black. Steve even found a black baseball cap. We crept downstairs and into the backyard. We decided not to risk using flashlights.

We moved along the path slowly. We didn't want to make a sound. We wanted to surprise them.

It seemed as if it took forever but we finally reached the clearing.

Please let them still be there, I thought. *Please. Please. Please.*

I peered up at the tree house. And spotted a light on the first level.

Yes!

As we tiptoed closer to the tree house, every

sound thundered in my ears. My sneakers squeaking on the wet grass. Steve's breathing. My heart pounding.

Don't let them hear us, I thought. *Not now. Not when we're so close.*

We made it to the big rock next to the old oak and ducked behind it. I motioned to Steve that I would go up the ladder first. He'd follow right behind.

I carefully climbed the ladder. I made sure I had my weight balanced and my hands positioned on each rung before I took the next step. We were so close to success—I didn't want to ruin everything now.

One rung. Two. Three. Four. Only one more to go.

I climbed to the fifth rung.

I carefully reached up to the trapdoor.

I made sure I had a firm grip on it.

I glanced down to make sure Steve was in position behind me.

Then I flung open the door. And burst into the tree house with a loud howl.

But what I saw made me scream in terror.

I thought I would scream forever.

16

A ghost.

A real ghost.

It looked like a boy. A boy about my age. But I could see right through him.

As I leaped up through the trapdoor, he reached out to grab me. His icy fingers brushed my cheek.

I dodged his grasp and flung myself against the wall.

And then Steve jumped up into the tree house, howling his special werewolf howl. It turned into a whine when he spotted the ghost.

The ghost extended both his arms straight out. His hands were clenched in tight fists. I watched in horror as he slowly uncurled his fingers and pointed them at Steve.

A gust of icy wind blew up—up from the ghost's hands. It swept Steve off his feet and sent him *whooshing* toward me.

Then there was a loud *thud!* The thud of the trapdoor slamming shut.

Steve and I huddled together in the corner. I was sweating even though the room was freezing cold. Beads of sweat dripped down my forehead and into my eyes. I wanted to blink. But I didn't dare.

I didn't dare take my eyes off the ghost.

The ghost started to move toward us. He seemed to walk, but his feet never really touched the floor.

His eyes—his glowing red eyes—stared into mine. I lifted my hand to wipe the sweat from my forehead. The ghost's eyes flickered. I dropped my hand down to my side—fast.

I could feel Steve trembling beside me. "Wh-what do you think he's going to do?" he whispered.

I didn't answer. I couldn't. All I could do was stare. Stare into those terrifying eyes.

The ghost moved closer.

Closer.

He lifted his filmy white arms and began to reach out. Reach out for us.

His lips parted in an evil sneer.

The air around us grew colder. My teeth began to chatter.

Closer. Closer.

He was inches from us now.

Do something, do something, I told myself. Don't just stand there. *DO SOMETHING!*

I leaped around the ghost and lunged across the room. Across to the trapdoor.

I slid on my stomach and grabbed for the handle. I began to pull, but it slipped out of my sweaty hand.

The ghost howled in fury. He rose up in the air.

I scrambled up on my knees and grabbed the handle again.

"Hurry, Dylan!" Steve screamed. "Hurry!"

The ghost swooped down.

I jerked the door open.

The ghost flew right at me. Then he flew right through me. He hovered over my head. I froze in sheer terror.

I stared up into his eyes. They glowed an angry red.

He floated close to me. I could feel his icy breath on my neck. Then he reached down and banged the trapdoor hard. It slammed shut.

"Don't move," he howled. "You're not going anywhere ever again."

17

"**Y**ou're not going anywhere ever again," the ghost repeated. "I can't let you leave. Not yet."

I shot a glance at Steve, but he sat shriveled up in the corner. His mouth gaped open and his hands and legs trembled. *He's not going to be much help here,* I thought.

"What do you want?" I managed to ask.

"I need your help," the ghost said.

"Help? What help? Who are you?" I was actually talking to a ghost!

He looked just like a regular kid. A regular kid I could see right through.

"My name is Corey—or it was Corey when I was alive. . . ." the ghost replied softly.

When I was alive.

"So you're really a ghost," I said to Corey—but I was staring at Steve.

"How does it feel to be a ghost?" I blurted out. I had so many questions. Now was my chance to get some answers. Especially since the ghost wasn't letting us go anywhere.

"I guess it feels like being asleep," he began to explain. "I'm not exactly sure. You see, this is my first day as a ghost. Before this I was trapped in this tree house—without any shape at all. But you changed all that."

"I-I did?" I asked.

"Yes," the ghost replied. "The more you worked on the tree house, the stronger I grew. Now I can move around. I can see again. I haven't been able to do that since I died. And I have a voice and a body—well, sort of a body. But I still can't leave the tree house. I'm still too weak."

"H-how did you become a ghost?" I asked.

"I died in this tree house," he replied. "In a lightning storm."

"Wow! Steve, did you hear that? The story is true," I cried.

Steve didn't say anything. To tell you the truth, I think he was in shock.

But I wasn't afraid at all. The ghost didn't seem scary. He just seemed sad. Sad and lonely.

"You said you need our help," I whispered. "What do you want us to do?"

"I want you to finish building the tree house," the ghost explained. "I've been trapped in this tree house where I died—for years and years. But if you finish the tree house, I'm sure I'll be strong enough to leave here."

That's all? That's easy! It's almost finished anyway, I thought.

"Will you help me?" the ghost asked again.

"Yeah. We'll help you," Steve interrupted before I could answer. "But we want to make a deal."

"A deal?" The ghost boy's voice sounded cold and hard. He floated over to Steve—and seeing him hover in the air made my body clench with fear.

"Why should I make a deal with *you?*" he bellowed.

86

18

I couldn't believe it! I'd been doing all the talking while my very mature brother hid in the corner. And now he wanted to make a deal!

Steve's going to ruin everything. We'll never get out of here alive.

I glared at Steve. "We don't have to make—"

Steve cut me off again. "We'll help you on one condition," he declared. "You have to help us get even with two girls."

"And you'll finish the tree house—no delays?" the ghost said.

"Yes," I said eagerly.

"Then I will help you," the ghost said.

"Deal," Steve replied. "Now here's the plan. . . ."

The next week Steve and I worked every day after school on the tree house.

Steve didn't read one comic book.

He didn't make one trip back to the house for Cheese Curlies.

I didn't even have to bribe him with doughnuts.

And now it was Saturday—and we were just about finished. The tree house looked awesome.

"Steve, I need some more nails," I called from the roof.

"Here, Dylan. Catch!" Steve threw a handful of nails at me. They flew over the roof and landed on the ground. Steve was turning back into his old self.

"Why do you have to act like such a jerk?" I shouted.

"Dylan, my lad, I can't wait until we're finished with the tree house. Then I'll never have to see you again."

"We still share a room," I replied.

"Not for long," Steve answered.

"Why?" I asked. "Are you going somewhere?"

"Nope," Steve answered. "You are."

"I don't think so, Steve."

"Oh, yes, you are. It's part of the deal I made with the ghost. You're moving into the tree house.

88

Corey needs someone to take over haunting the tree house. I told him you would do it. You like ghosts so much, I figured you wouldn't mind becoming one."

"How could you do this to me?" I yelled. "I'm not doing it!"

"A deal's a deal, Dylan, my lad," Steve answered. Then he started to laugh. "Boy, you'll believe anything!"

I was ready to throw my hammer at Steve, but I stopped when I heard voices down below.

Girls' voices.

Betsy and Kate.

"They're here," I whispered to Steve.

"I knew they would show up," Steve whispered back.

"Wow!" Kate said as she and Betsy approached the old oak. "The tree house is almost finished."

"Yeah. Your dumb tricks didn't work," I mumbled under my breath.

Kate and Betsy walked around the tree house slowly, studying it. "It looks really good," Kate finally said. "I'll bet this is what it looked like when it was first built."

Betsy nodded. "It's not bad," she said. "But you're lucky you didn't get hurt."

I opened my mouth to start to tell them off. But Kate cut me off.

"Maybe those terrible stories we heard weren't true. Maybe someone was trying to trick us," she said.

Yeah. Sure. Right, I thought.

"Listen," Steve said. "Why don't the four of us try to be friends from now on? We're going to have a party up here tonight. To celebrate finishing the tree house. Want to come?"

Kate and Betsy didn't answer right away. Kate started nibbling on her ponytail.

"Sure," Betsy finally agreed.

"Great," Steve said. "We'll meet here after dark. It'll be fun!"

The girls left.

Steve and I finished hammering in the last nails on the tree house roof. Then we climbed down and inspected our work from every angle.

The tree house looked really awesome!

We dashed home, gulped down dinner, and collected stuff for the party—chips, soda, things like that.

As soon as it grew dark out, we headed back through the woods. I had gotten used to it being so quiet out here. The Fear Street Woods didn't frighten me anymore.

Steve and I climbed the ladder and set out everything for the party.

Steve popped a Cheese Curlie in his mouth and

walked over to the tree house window. "Here they come!" he whispered.

We could hear the girls climbing the ladder. Steve pulled open the trapdoor for them. "Come on in," he called.

Betsy peeked her head through the door first. Kate was right behind her.

"What do you think?" I asked as they glanced around the first level.

Betsy remained silent. Kate's eyes looked as if they were about to pop right out of her head. "Wow! It really turned out great," she finally said.

The girls plopped down on the floor. I started to pour soda for everyone.

And that's when we heard it.

A soft moan.

"Wh-what was that?" Kate asked.

"Probably just the wind," Steve replied.

Then we heard it again.

Louder this time. And creepier. Almost like a wail.

Betsy grabbed Kate's hand. "We're leaving," she declared.

She moved to the trapdoor, bent down, and grasped its handle.

But before she could pull it open, an icy wind blew through the tree house, sending everything soaring through the air.

The chips whirled around the room. Cups of soda flew up and splattered against the wall.

Steve and I braced ourselves on the floor.

Betsy's knuckles turned white as she gripped the trapdoor handle. Her eyes were wide with fright.

And then Corey sprang up—right through the trapdoor. He let out the most hideous shriek I've ever heard.

The girls screamed their heads off.

Corey stretched himself to twice his normal size. He really was much stronger—now that we'd finished the house for him.

He swung his filmy arms wildly and the icy wind blew stronger. His eyes glowed like red embers. And his mouth gaped open—showing rows and rows of rotted, black teeth.

Steve laughed like a maniac. His plan had worked—the girls were getting the worst scare of their lives.

I stared at the girls as they shrieked and shrieked. They couldn't stop.

And then I saw something.

Something that made my breath catch in my throat.

Something that made my heart stop.

19

Betsy and Kate rose up in the air.

Up to join Corey.

As I watched, the color faded from their bodies. Their black hair turned a misty white. Their eyes began to glow a deep red.

My heart pounded. I thought my chest was going to explode.

The girls wrapped their arms around Corey. And they hugged!

"They're ghosts, too!" I howled. "They're ghosts, too!"

Steve raised his eyes to the weird scene. I heard him give a low groan.

The three ghosts cackled and danced in the air. They spun around and around.

Cold air shot through me as they flew past. My teeth started to chatter.

"Run!" Steve screamed. "Run!"

I flung open the trapdoor.

As we slid down the trunk I could feel my skin ripping open against the rough bark. It didn't matter. Nothing mattered except getting away— fast.

We bolted across the clearing toward the woods. We nearly reached the path.

And then the ghosts swooped down on us.

They joined hands and surrounded us. Surrounded us in an icy circle of air.

My whole body trembled as the ghosts whirled around us. Faster and faster. And laughing—evil, hideous laughs.

Corey swung in front of me and grinned in triumph.

And then the ghosts began to move in.

Closer and closer.

Tightening the circle.

Until we were trapped.

20

"**W**e have to get out of here—now!" I screamed to Steve.

Steve and I flung ourselves at the ghosts. But the ghosts bounced us right back. Back to the center of the circle.

I tried again. I flew at the filmy creatures with all my might.

This time they caught me. I was stuck right between two quivering, icy ghosts. I felt as if I were being smothered in freezing-cold Jell-O.

I started to shiver. My arms and legs shook and my teeth chattered. My lips began to turn numb.

I couldn't breathe. I started to choke. I was freezing. Freezing to death.

It was all a trick, I thought. A horrible trick. Corey made us finish the tree house. And now he's going to kill us.

Steve sank to the ground and curled up in a little ball. I clenched my fists and threw myself against the ghosts. I pushed and pushed. Then with one last burst of strength, I shoved against them hard.

I was out! I doubled over, gulping down air. I could breathe again. And I was free!

I straightened up—and that's when I realized the awful truth. I was still inside the circle.

"You can't keep me here!" I screamed, running forward again—pushing against the clammy cold that surrounded me.

Betsy shrieked with laughter. Corey laughed, too.

"Stop! Stop! Can't you see they're scared?" It was Kate.

The laughter died.

Then Betsy spoke.

"I'm sorry," she said. "We were just playing. We didn't mean to scare you."

"Yeah," Corey added. "I guess we got carried away."

Carried away? This must be a bad dream, I thought. A really bad dream.

"Corey is our brother," Kate began. "We thought we would never find him."

My mouth dropped open.

I glanced at Steve. He sat shriveled up on the ground, staring into space.

"Corey, Betsy, and I were the three kids in the tree house—the kids we told you about," Kate continued. "When the tree house was hit by lightning, Betsy and I were on one side of it. Corey was on the other side."

"We all died at the same time," Betsy said, taking up the story. "When we became ghosts, Kate and I were together. But Corey disappeared. His spirit was lost. We've been searching for him ever since."

Kate waited for me to say something. But I didn't. I was afraid to speak. I was afraid to move. I was too afraid to do anything but listen.

"When you discovered the tree house," she went on, "we suddenly found ourselves back in these woods. We *thought* we had been brought back to scare you away from it. So you wouldn't get hurt—the way we did."

"But now we know we were wrong," Betsy interrupted. "We must have been brought back to find Corey. And you two helped us!"

"Thank you. Thank you so much," Corey added. "You freed me from the tree house. Finally!"

"Yes!" Betsy exclaimed. "We would never have found Corey without you!"

As she spoke a ray of moonlight broke through

the thick treetops. It cast a golden glow on the three ghosts.

"I-I guess I believe you," I stammered.

"We're telling the truth," Kate replied. "Really."

"I-I guess this could be kind of cool," I stuttered. "You'll be able to tell me everything I ever wanted to know about ghosts. I can come out to the tree house every day and you can—"

"Sorry, Dylan," Corey interrupted me. "We've been stuck on earth a long time. You brought us together. Now we can leave."

And with that, the beam of moonlight began to shimmer. Steve and I watched in awe as it expanded to form a wide, sparkling bridge. It stretched from the moon all the way down to the clearing. It was the most beautiful thing I had ever seen.

The three ghosts reached out and touched Steve and me one last time. Their fingers felt soft and fluttery, like a gentle breeze. As we looked at them, they started to fade and become even more transparent.

Then they joined hands and stepped onto the bridge of light. Kate glanced back and waved.

They walked on the shimmering moonbeam.

Up toward the sky.

And then they disappeared.

"Can you believe that?" I asked Steve. "Can you believe that!"

Steve still couldn't speak. But he did manage to nod "yes."

"Well, well, well, Steve, my lad. You finally believe in ghosts!"

21

I felt dazed after the ghosts disappeared. I turned and followed Steve home. With our three friends gone, I also felt strange. Kind of alone.

I walked close to Steve. The woods seemed darker than ever.

Twigs crackled loudly under our shoes. I heard animal moans and strange cries.

Steve stopped. He spun around. "Hey—where are we?"

Nothing looked familiar. "I-I think we went the wrong way," I stammered. I searched for the moon, but trees blocked the light.

"Those ghosts got me all mixed up," Steve

confessed. He turned and pointed. "I think the path is over there."

I followed him, but I couldn't see any path.

Then, in a small, round clearing, I saw a strange sight. Silvery moonlight spilled into the clearing. And in the moonlight, I saw an old swing set. An old-fashioned wooden swing and slide. Worn and rickety-looking.

And on top of the swing set sat a boy. He had long blond curls that shone in the moonlight. He was dressed in a sailor suit, the kind you see kids wearing in very old pictures.

He was so pale. The moonlight seemed to pour right through him.

Was he stuck up there on that battered swing set?

"Help me," he called when Steve and I stepped into the clearing, into the spotlight of silvery moonlight. "Please—help me!"

Steve and I both rolled our eyes and shook our heads. "Here we go again!" I moaned.

GHOSTS of FEAR STREET ®

FRIGHT KNIGHT

"More blood!" I ordered. I slowly stepped back from the guillotine.

I gazed down at the body kneeling at the bottom of the guillotine. His hands were tied behind his back. I spotted the head on the floor, a few feet away.

The blank eyes stared up at me. The mouth gaped open, frozen in a scream of terror.

I walked over and nudged it with the toe of my sneaker.

"This is nowhere near scary enough," I said.

"Right you are, Mike." Mr. Spellman squirted more fake blood on the wax dummy. A long stream of the sticky red stuff dribbled over the gleaming steel blade of the guillotine.

It looked great—just right for the Museum of History's Mysteries.

"Yu-u-uck!" My sister, Carly, let out one of her earsplitting squeals. She'd been so quiet I had almost forgotten she existed.

No such luck.

She started to jump down from her seat on the old mummy case. Salem, our big black cat, leaped off her lap with an angry meow. Then Carly's feet hit the floor.

"You guys are gross!" She gave us the famous Carly look and rolled her eyes.

Carly has the same blue eyes as me. Her hair is shoulder length and mine is buzzed short for the summer. But it's the same hair. Red. We even have the same freckles all over our noses and cheeks.

My dad has red hair, too. In the pictures I've seen, my mother had brown hair and was kind of small, like me. I don't remember our mom at all. She died when we were really little. For as long as I can remember there's just been Dad, Carly, and me.

I'm twelve and Carly is eleven. We're practically the same height, too. A lot of people think we're twins.

It's enough to make a guy hurl.

My dad says not to worry. Girls grow faster than boys. He promised that someday I'll tower over her.

I dream of that day.

"How can you get so excited over something so

gross?" Carly shivered. "All that phony blood. It's . . .
it's—"

"Terrific!" Dad ran into the room. I could tell that
he had been dusting the mummies again. Big gunky
cobwebs trailed from his clothes. Clouds of dust
puffed out of his red hair.

Dad dashed over to the guillotine. He checked it
from every angle. His grin grew wider and wider.
"Excellent work!"

Mr. Spellman smiled proudly. He took his job as
museum caretaker very seriously. Dad gave me and
Mr. Spellman the thumbs-up. "But maybe just a little
more blood . . ." he added.

Dad took the plastic bottle and squirted a red
puddle all around the head. When he was done, he
nodded. "Perfect! It's really horrible now."

"Way to go, Dad," I said.

Carly made a soft gagging sound.

He looked right at her. "Don't forget, scary is
exactly why people come to Fear Street." Dad's hands
were covered with fake blood. He scratched his ear,
and a red glob smeared across his face.

Cool! The blood looked even creepier on a live
person than it did on a wax dummy. And it will look
totally awesome smeared all over me on Halloween.

"That's why the Museum of History's Mysteries is
such a stroke of genius." Dad glanced around the old
place and smiled.

3

"I can't fail. Not this time," Dad vowed. "This is the perfect business for Fear Street. It's why we decided to move here to Shadyside in the first place."

I thought back and remembered—remembered the very night Dad got his great brainstorm to move here and open the museum.

So many weird things happen in Shadyside that the town was on the news almost every night. Dad figured people would want to come here and find out for themselves if the stories were true. Which made it the perfect place for a scary museum.

"Where else could you find ghosts playing hide-and-seek in the cemetery?" Dad asked, thinking back to a recent ghost sighting.

"And don't forget that haunted tree house in the woods," Mr. Spellman added.

Dad sighed. "How could I ever forget that?"

I know Mr. Spellman tries to be helpful. But reminding Dad about my friend Dylan and his haunted tree house only made Dad sad. He had missed out on meeting any of the ghosts and was still sort of bummed out about it.

"All we need is something special that people will be . . . well, dying to see." He chuckled at his own joke. "Then people will come. And the Museum of History's Mysteries will be a big success."

"You mean like the alien tracking station you set up

in Grandpa Conway's backyard, Dad?" Carly whined. She didn't give Dad time to answer. She went right on whining.

"Or that freaky petting farm you bought? Let's see—there was the two-headed llama and that stupid unicorn. Couldn't you tell it was a goat with a cardboard horn tied to its head?"

Dad cringed. "I almost forgot about that one," he admitted. "Hey, I thought it was real. Everybody did. It looked real, didn't it, Mike?"

"It looked real to me," I agreed.

Carly made a really mean face at me. I call it her rodent face. It was one of the things she did best.

But I made a better face back at her.

"I think it's going to be great," I said. "All my friends say this place is totally awesome."

"Totally awesome—" Carly imitated me in a squeaky little voice. "Bunch of nerds," she mumbled to herself.

I glared at her. But before I could answer, she turned to my dad again.

"Come on, Dad. What normal kid wants to live in a place that has mummies in the living room and coffins in the dining room and catapults and swords in the kitchen?" she complained.

"How would *you* know what normal kids like, Carly?" I asked.

5

Besides, she wasn't even right. Well, not exactly. All those things were in what used to be the living room and the dining room and the kitchen. That was before Dad turned the downstairs of the big old house into the museum.

We lived upstairs. Our living room, dining room, and kitchen were pretty ordinary compared to down here.

"All right, you two." Dad stepped between us. "No time to fight. Halloween is only two short weeks away. And Shadyside will be crawling with tourists. We've got to be ready for them. We haven't had many customers yet. But Halloween's the perfect time to improve our business." Behind his black-framed glasses Dad's eyes grew serious. I knew what the look meant. He was worried. "They'd better come," he added very quietly. "Or I will have to close."

I knew the thought of closing the museum made Dad sad. It made Mr. Spellman and me sad, too. The Museum of History's Mysteries was a one-and-only kind of place. A place where people could see all sorts of great, spooky stuff. Wax dummies lurked in the basement in the Hall of Wax. Terrifying instruments of torture hung on the back porch. A totally awesome bunch of medieval weapons decorated the front hall. There was no place like it in the whole world.

"Don't worry, Dad," I said. "People will line up and

6

down the street when that special exhibit gets here from England."

Dad cheered up in a flash. "That's right! Uncle Basil sent it weeks ago. It should be here any day. I can't wait. Imagine how lucky we are! Owning our very own suit of armor!"

I couldn't wait, either. I'm crazy about knights in armor. That was one of the main reasons Mr. Spellman and I were such good friends. He could hardly stop talking about them.

Mr. Spellman worked as the caretaker of the museum since it opened. We have been real close ever since. I couldn't guess his age, but he looked way older than Dad. He was tall and thin. He wore his white hair long, and he had a bushy white mustache. His bright blue eyes lit up whenever he talked about his favorite subjects. Like guillotines or how mummies were made.

He knew everything about really important stuff like that.

Most important, he knew all about knights and swords and castles and dragons.

We talked about knights for hours. He taught me the names of all the weapons—and all about the rules of chivalry. The rules of chivalry told a knight how to behave. How to fight fair. How to be a brave knight.

Mr. Spellman walked over to me and smiled. "And

don't forget," he reminded us, "in his letter, Basil said he was sending along something extra special just for Mike."

Carly didn't need to be reminded. Uncle Basil wasn't sending a present for her.

Her face got all puckery. Like the time we had a contest to see who could eat a whole lemon.

Carly won.

"Aren't you guys forgetting what else Uncle Basil said? That suit of armor is supposed to be haunted!"

"I sure hope so. That's the best thing about it, Carly." Dad wiped the fake blood from his hands with an old rag. "If it is haunted, we're sitting on a gold mine!"

A shiver skipped up my back. The kind of trembly feeling I always felt waiting for something great. My birthday. Or the last day of school.

Or when I felt scared.

But I wasn't scared. I just felt excited. Yeah, that was it. That's why I had a weird, jumpy feeling in my stomach. Sort of like I'd accidentally swallowed a live bug.

"Mr. Conway?" someone called from the front porch. The guy sounded nervous. A lot of delivery and repair people did when they came to the Museum of History's Mysteries. "It's Stanley's Moving and Storage. Got a delivery here for you!"

We all raced out to the front porch. I spotted a giant

moving van parked in front of our house. Two delivery men were pulling a huge crate out of the back. I skidded to a stop in the middle of the porch. Carly slammed into my back. She peered over my shoulder to see what was going on.

The wooden crate had a long, rectangular shape. The rough, dark wood looked very old and knotty. A few of the planks were warped and cracked.

I saw strange-looking stamps all over it. The printing on them looked weird, with strange, twisted letters that I could hardly read. But one big stamp that I could read said FRAGILE in bold red letters.

The delivery men tipped the crate on its side to stand it up. It towered over them.

Dad and Mr. Spellman walked all around it. I scrambled over to them. Carly followed me.

The two delivery guys grunted as they hoisted the crate up on their shoulders. From down where I stood, it looked bigger than ever.

"It's the armor, isn't it?" I asked. I peered through the cracks between the planks of wood, but I couldn't see a thing. I hopped up and down. I couldn't help it. Dad didn't have to answer. I knew his answer from the smile on his face.

"Now be careful. Not too fast. Easy does it, fellas." Dad directed them. "Carry it over to the front porch. We'll drag it inside from there. Carly, out of the way. Mike, you'd better be careful. Not so close. You'll—"

9

Dad's last words vanished in a kind of choking sound as something sliced through the crate. It gleamed in the sunlight.

It was a giant ax. A knight's battle-ax.

And it came right at me.

The huge blade zipped through the air. As if an invisible hand had taken aim. The blade fell down.

I screamed and jumped out of the way.

But not far enough.

2

"My foot! My foot!"

I took a deep breath. I felt like I was going to hurl.
Then I moved my foot. I wiggled my toes.

My toes?

I forced myself to look down.

The ax blade stuck into the ground. On one side I
saw the white rubber toe of my sneaker. On the other
side, I saw the rest of my foot.

"Heh, look—" I moved my foot away from the ax. I
poked my toes through the hole in my sneaker and
wiggled them wildly. They were still attached. All five
of them.

My father sighed. A long sigh of relief. I grinned at
him.

11

"It's just the rubber from the shoe, Dad. My toes are fine."

The battle-ax had sliced off the front of my shoe, but I had pulled back my toes just in time. Lucky break for me.

"You've got to be more careful, Mike." Dad slapped my back in that friendly sort of way he always did when he was worried and he didn't want me to know it. "Why don't you go inside and change your shoes."

I didn't want to. I didn't want to miss a second of the excitement. Before I had a chance to start griping, Mr. Spellman put a hand on my shoulder.

"Come on," he said. "Race you to the house."

That was all I needed to hear. I hurried up the steps to the house. I shot under the sign above the door that said MUSEUM OF HISTORY'S MYSTERIES in creepy-looking red letters on a black background. I shoved open the front door and skidded to the right, all set to bolt up the stairs.

I didn't need to. My old sneakers sat on the landing at the bottom of the steps. Right where I was never supposed to leave them.

Mr. Spellman came huffing and puffing into the house. I already had my chopped-up shoes off. I slipped on my old ones.

"Slower than a snail!"

I always said that to Mr. Spellman when I beat him in a race. He usually laughed.

He didn't this time. I don't think he even heard me.

Mr. Spellman looked really excited. His blue eyes lit up. His smile made his bushy white mustache twitch. He plunked down on the step next to me. "Did you see what I saw?" he asked.

He glanced over at the front door. Through the open door we saw Stanley and the other delivery guy coming up the steps with the crate. "Did you read the shipping labels on that crate?"

"Uh, no," I told Mr. Spellman.

"You didn't read them!" he exclaimed in disbelief.

"Give me a break. It's hard to start reading shipping labels when a great big battle-ax is about to split you in two."

"Okay, okay. Those labels say that the armor was shipped from Dreadbury Castle." Mr. Spellman rubbed his hands together. "This is even better than I thought, Mike. Much better."

"It is?"

"If I remember my history right . . ." Thinking really hard, Mr. Spellman squeezed his eyes shut. "Yes. That's right. That's it!" He hopped to his feet. "Dreadbury Castle was the home of Sir Thomas Barlayne!"

He announced the name as if it was supposed to mean something to me.

It didn't.

Mr. Spellman shook his head. "Don't you remember the story of Sir Thomas Barlayne? Sir Thomas was an evil knight. A wicked knight. Some say he was the most wicked knight who ever lived. Finally a noble wizard cast a spell on Sir Thomas. He trapped the wicked knight inside his suit of armor forever."

I stood up. "But that's good, isn't it? That's just what Dad wants. A haunted suit of armor for the museum."

"Yes, that's what your dad wants." Some of the excitement faded from Mr. Spellman's eyes. His voice dropped low. "I wonder if he knows the rest of the story."

He might have been talking to himself, but he sure got my attention.

I grabbed Mr. Spellman's sleeve and tugged. "Rest of what story?"

Mr. Spellman laughed. "Oh, nothing much," he said. He waved away my question with one hand. "It's just some silly old story. According to the legend, whoever owns Sir Thomas's armor is cursed. He's doomed to bad luck—or worse!"

"Worse?" The word squeaked out of me. Bad luck, I could imagine. I could picture getting F's on math tests even though I studied. I could imagine my friend Pete telling the whole world I had a crush on Sara Medlow. And I sure could picture being Carly's brother.

All that was bad luck.

But worse?

"But if the legend is true, won't that be great for the museum?"

Mr. Spellman looked down at me. His eyes twinkled. His mustache twitched. "Maybe not so great for us, huh?"

He bent down so that he could look right into my eyes. "I'll tell you what, Mike. Let's keep this our secret, okay? There's no use worrying your dad. And we don't want to scare Carly. If the armor is haunted . . ."

He straightened up and looked out the window. "What do you say we play detective?"

"You mean we'll check it out together?"

Mr. Spellman nodded.

"Excellent!" He slapped me a high five. "And don't worry, Mr. Spellman," I told him. "I'll watch out for you."

"And I"—Mr. Spellman ruffled my hair—"will watch out for you. Deal?"

"Deal!"

We walked outside onto the porch together. We both smiled about our secret pact. I saw the delivery guys climbing back into their truck. Then I saw the crate stretched out beside me.

Dad didn't waste any time. Holding a crowbar, he crouched down next to the crate. He slipped the edge of the bar under the crate's lid and pushed. I heard a squeaking sound as the nails that held the lid in place came loose.

As Dad pushed up with the crowbar, Mr. Spellman grabbed the edge of the lid and pulled. Carly stood to one side. She was pretending she didn't care much. But I noticed that she was chewing on her lower lip. Her nervous habit.

I sort of hopped around the crate in the circle. I felt so excited I couldn't keep still.

Finally Dad and Mr. Spellman lifted the lid off the crate. I scooted forward. I held my breath. Carly stood right next to me.

We all leaned over and peered inside.

All I saw were piles and piles of fluffy stuff. Shredded newspaper.

"It's paper." Carly sounded as disappointed as I felt.

Dad grinned. "Not just paper, Carly," he said. "Go ahead. Reach in there and see what you can find."

"Me?" Carly squeaked.

"Are you afraid?" Dad asked.

"No way," she said. I could tell she was scared silly. But acting like everything was cool.

The long crate suddenly reminded me of a coffin. I wondered if Carly had the same idea, too.

Her mouth twitched. She pushed up the sleeve of her blue sweater. She reached into the crate. Her arm disappeared into the mountains of paper shreds.

The paper rustled as she felt around for something solid. I saw her lean over and reach in even deeper.

"I think I feel something," she told us.

Then she screamed.

"It's got me! It's grabbed me! Help!"

I watched Carly try and try again to yank her arm out.

But something—or someone—had grabbed her. And it wouldn't let go.

3

Carly tugged and squirmed. Her face turned red. Dad and Mr. Spellman started digging. Shredded newspaper flew in all directions.

"Hold on now, honey," Dad said.

"Hurry! It's got me," she wailed.

She was out of control. Even I felt sorry for her. Well, almost.

Dad pulled up her arm. The fingers of a metal hand were wrapped around Carly's wrist.

"Well, would you look at this," Dad said. He laughed. The metal hand was attached to a long metal arm.

"Your bracelet got caught," Dad said. "Hold still. I'll have you unhooked in a second." He pried the metal fingers open one by one. Carly snatched back her hand.

The metal hand and arm dropped back into the crate with a clunk.

"Stupid armor," Carly grumbled. She looked down at her wrist, rubbing it.

I looked over my shoulder at Mr. Spellman. I rolled my eyes. He rolled his, too.

Dad reached in and pulled out another piece. "Now look at this," he said.

Smiling, Dad held up a helmet. The last rays of the setting sun glinted against the metal, turning it glowing red. Hot. Fiery.

My mouth fell open. I didn't even realize I was holding my breath until I let it go. "Cool! It's so cool."

Then Dad handed the helmet to me. Just looking at the helmet was nothing compared to touching it.

I ran my hands over it. It felt heavier than I thought it would. And not cold. Not like metal should be. It felt warm. The way it would be if somebody had just taken it off.

A shiver crawled up my back. I cradled the helmet in my arms. Dad pulled a metal shin guard out of the crate and set it on the floor. A metal foot guard came next.

Dad's eyes gleamed. He reached into the pile of shredded paper for another piece of the armor. "This is it! Our chance at fame and fortune. This is going to be the best and the spookiest exhibit anyone has ever seen. On Fear Street or any place else. People will come from all over the world to see it and—"

His words stopped suddenly. His sandy-colored eyebrows drew together as he frowned. He kept moving his hand around under the shredded paper. He felt around for something way down at the bottom of the crate.

"What's this?" Dad pulled his arm out. He held up something bright and shiny. The strange round object dangled at the end of a long golden chain.

It looked like a giant marble, but weirder looking than any marble I had ever seen.

Inside the marble strange blue smoke spiraled and swirled. Dark blue. Light blue. Sparkling silvery flecks whirled slowly around in the smoke, like tiny shooting stars.

I grabbed for it.

So did Carly.

So did Mr. Spellman.

I got there first.

"Slower than snails!" I grinned at them, the pendant in my hands. "This must be my special surprise from Uncle Basil!" I slipped the chain over my neck before anybody else had a chance to touch it. I stared down at the pendant dangling against my white T-shirt. "Gee—it looks cool, doesn't it?"

Dad agreed. So did Carly. She sounded jealous. That made me like the pendant even more.

Mr. Spellman stepped forward. "If you ask me," he said, looking at the pendant, "it looks positively magical."

"Yeah, it does sort of, doesn't it?" I nodded.

A magic pendant.

It was the best surprise I'd had since Dad took us to New York City last year to buy a new mummy.

We all watched as Dad finished unpacking the crate. We gathered up the armor and took it into the front hall.

Mr. Spellman and I handed Dad the pieces. Piece by piece, he slowly put Sir Thomas together.

Carly stood by, holding Salem in her arms. I could tell she didn't want to touch the armor.

When Dad finished, we all stood back and took a good look.

Sir Thomas's armor could have easily fit my favorite pro wrestler, Hulk Hooligan. The shoulders were about a yard wide. The legs were round and solid. They reminded me of small tree trunks. About three of me could have hidden behind the breastplate, no problem.

I thought about all the stories in all my books about castles and knights.

"Awesome!" I let out the word at the end of a sigh.

"He does look awesome, doesn't he?" Mr. Spellman clapped me on the back.

Dad smiled. "Now all we have to do is keep our fingers crossed. If we're lucky, this old pile of metal really is haunted. And that will bring the customers running!"

The phone rang and Dad went to answer it. Mr. Spellman hurried out, too. He said he had some work to do down in the wax museum. When they were gone, Carly edged up real close to me.

"What do you think, Mikey?" She always calls me Mikey when she tries to make me mad. "Are you scared the armor might really be haunted?"

"The only thing I'm scared of is your ugly face!" I gave her a playful punch on the arm. Then I dashed out of the hall and up the stairs.

It was my turn to start dinner. I knew exactly what I was going to make—macaroni and cheese, the food Carly hated more than anything in the whole wide world.

It was Carly's turn to do the dishes. I made sure I cooked the macaroni and cheese just a little too long. So after dinner she had to scrape all the hard pieces off the bottom of the pan. While she was doing that and grumbling to herself, I hurried to my room.

I still had a school project to do about polar bears. I had to read the report to my class tomorrow. Also my favorite TV show, *Scream Theater,* was on at nine.

I did my homework, but I never got a chance to watch *Scream Theater.* It had been a big day. I was beat.

I brushed my teeth, pulled on my pajamas, and fell into bed.

But I kept my pendant on. Stretched out in bed, I held it up in front of my face. I watched the curling blue smoke glimmer in the moonlight that slipped through my window blinds.

I got this weird feeling that the smoke was hiding something. Something really great. I tried to get a closer look. But the more I looked, the more the color swirled.

I fell asleep before I knew it.

Thump. Thump.

I was dreaming about something. I couldn't remember what. I thought it had something to do with polar bears. And blue marbles. And knights in shining armor.

Thump. Thump.

There it was again.

I opened my eyes and listened.

Thump. Thump.

Definitely not part of my dream.

I sat up and held my breath.

23

Thump. Thump.

It came from downstairs.

Thump. Thump.

I swung my legs over the side of the bed. I sat with my head tilted, listening closer.

Thump. Thump.

I couldn't think of anything down in the museum that made that kind of noise.

At least, not before tonight.

Thump. Thump.

I stood up. My legs felt a little rubbery.

Only one thing could be making the noise.

The armor.

Thump. Thump.

I gulped and hurried downstairs. The museum kitchen was right under my room. The closer I got to it, the louder it sounded.

Thump. Thump.

I gazed down at my pendant. The swirling blue smoke pulsed to the rhythm of the sounds.

Thump. Thump.

I moved through the museum, following the sound. At the door to the kitchen, I stopped. I gulped for air, the way I do in gym class when Mr. Sirk, our PE teacher, makes us run extra laps.

This was it! My chance to catch a ghost in action. My chance to prove that the armor really was haunted!

24

Thump. Thump.

I took a deep breath. I pushed open the kitchen door.

Thump. Thump.

I took a couple of shaky steps inside.

Thump. Thump.

I squinted into the dark. And I saw it.

It was hideous.

I couldn't help it. I screamed.

4

"**C**arly! You creep!"

My jerky sister stood in the middle of the kitchen with a broom in her hands. She pounded on the ceiling with the handle.

I glared at her. "What do you think you're doing?"

I tried to keep my voice down. I didn't want to wake Dad.

Carly was doubled over laughing. She pointed at my face. "Look, it's the nerd patrol. Out ghost hunting."

Carly laughed some more. She can really crack herself up with her dumb jokes.

"Yeah, well, only a true jerk starts banging a broom handle on the ceiling in the middle of the night," I said.

I fingered my blue pendant. Now that the thumping had stopped, the pulsing had stopped, too. I closed my fingers around it.

"You're lucky Dad didn't wake up," I told her. "He would have thought the ghost had come for sure. He would have been so excited. Can you imagine how he would have felt when he found out it was only you?"

For once, Carly actually looked sorry. She put down the broom. "I guess I never thought of that," she said. "I just wanted to scare you."

"Well, you didn't." I crossed my arms over my chest. I tried to give her the same kind of look Dad gave us when we made him angry or disappointed. "You just caused trouble, that's all."

I suppose I should have considered myself lucky. I had actually seen Carly look sorry for once. I should have known it would never happen again.

"What's the matter, Mikey? Were you afraid of the big, bad knight down here?"

"Look who's talking. You're the one who thought it grabbed you," I reminded her. "O-o-oh! Help me! Help me!" I imitated her in a high-pitched, girl voice.

"Well, I'm not scared now," she said. She tossed her hair over one shoulder. "You're the one who believes in haunted armor."

"Well, what if the legend is true?" I asked her. "Do you want to meet the ghost of the most wicked knight who ever lived?"

"Oh, come on," Carly said. "You don't believe all that stuff? I mean, you don't think the armor could . . . could walk around or anything, do you?"

"There's only one way to find out."

Carly pretended that she didn't care about the haunted armor and the curse. But I could tell that deep down inside, she was scared.

But I wasn't scared.

"Come on." I grabbed her arm and pulled her out of the kitchen. "Let's go check it out."

As we left the kitchen and turned down the dark hallway, I started to get that creepy feeling again.

Not that I'm a chicken or anything. But the Museum of History's Mysteries can be sort of spooky. Especially at night.

In the moonlight that poured through the windows, our shadows looked all twisted and deformed. And things around the place you normally didn't notice, like a lamp or a big potted plant, looked a lot different in the dark—like they might reach out and grab you.

I heard a *squeak, squeak, squeak*. It sounded like fingernails on a blackboard. It made my skin crawl.

I stopped.

The noise stopped.

It was only the floor. I sighed.

I should have known. Everything around the museum always squeaks. It's part of what makes the big old house so much fun.

28

Except at night. When you're creeping through the place all alone with no one but your goofy sister. And you're looking for a haunted suit of armor.

We reached the dining room, where Dad's entire coffin collection is on display. He likes to call the room Coffin Central. He thinks that's pretty funny.

In the daytime it's a great place to play hide-and-seek.

But at night . . .

I heard a small hiccup. Then I realized I had made it. I glanced over at Carly, waiting for her to tease me.

But for once, Carly didn't say a word. I guess the room had creeped her out, too. She grabbed my hand. Her steps dragged.

I pulled her into the room. All the coffins were closed. Mr. Spellman always closed them before he went home at night.

What did it matter? Both of us knew what each and every one of them held.

The one next to us held a wax dummy of Dracula. Wooden stake through the heart and all.

The one over on our right had a wax dummy inside, too.

But the dummy had a mirror in place of a face. When you bent over the coffin and looked inside . . .

A shiver snaked its way up my back and over my shoulders. I walked a little faster.

"You're not scared, are you, Mikey?" This time

Carly wasn't teasing me. I could tell she was hoping I'd say no.

"No way." Was that me talking so tough? I tried to keep my voice steady. "There's nothing to be afraid of—

"Yow!" I let out a yelp of pain. Carly grabbed my arm.

"Mike? What? What?"

"I banged my knee on a coffin." Ouch. I rubbed my leg. "That hurts."

"Try not to be such a klutz," she whispered. "You'll wake up Dad."

"Try not to be such a chicken."

"Me? I'm not afraid of anything," she said.

"Except the haunted armor," I reminded her.

I kept walking, but Carly stopped in her tracks. I glanced back at her. She stood frozen to the spot. She peered into the shadows, twisting a strand of hair with her fingers.

"Maybe this isn't such a great idea after all. I mean . . ." Carly said in a shaky voice, "what if there really is a ghost? Maybe we should give him a few nights to sort of rest and get used to the place."

I didn't bother answering. Mostly because I hoped there *was* a ghost. And a curse. I wanted people to come to see Sir Thomas from miles around so we would make a zillion dollars and could live in the museum forever.

We finally made it through the coffin room and went into the living room. Even though Dad had spent the entire afternoon dusting the mummies, dust covered every inch of everything else. Clouds of dust drifted over the floor and blew around our feet as we walked.

That's exactly the way Dad likes it.

Dusty and musty. With cobwebs hanging off the walls like ghoulish party streamers.

As we crept across the floor, our slippers made a dull scraping sound. The sound a mummy might make dragging itself across the room.

Mr. Spellman always closed the coffins at night. But the mummies were always open for business.

Out of the corner of my eye I could see Dad's favorite mummy. The one he called Charlie. Charlie stood propped up in his case. His stiff arms jutted out in front of him. His sunken eyes stared across the darkness. Right at us.

I made a gulping sound and tried to cover it up with a cough.

"Race you the rest of the way!" I dropped Carly's hand. I sprinted into the parlor. Dad had set up the armor on a wooden stand just inside the doorway.

I beat Carly by a mile and stopped near the open door, waiting for her.

Finally she caught up. I grinned. "Slow as a snail!"

Carly didn't answer.

She stared over my shoulder. Her mouth dropped open.

She pointed.

I looked through the doorway and saw—nothing.

Empty space.

The armor was gone!

5

"**M**ike!" Carly's voice trembled. "Mike, where is he? Where is the knight?"

He had vanished all right. All that remained of him was his wooden stand.

"Do you know what this means?" I asked her.

"Yeah." Carly gulped. "The armor moved. It really is haunted."

"Right! The story is true!" I whispered. "Sir Thomas's ghost is in that armor. And he can move! He can walk!"

"He could be anywhere!" Carly croaked. "He could be hiding in the basement. He could be on his way upstairs." She took a step back into the mummy room. "He could be right in this room. Hiding in the dark."

I scanned the shadows. "I don't think so," I told her. "He's pretty big. I think we'd notice him. Let's look for him."

"Maybe he'll come back on his own," she replied in a shaky voice. "Like Salem does when he sneaks out of the house at night."

"Carly, get real. We're talking about a ghost, okay?"

I grabbed a handful of her robe and dragged her back the way we came. We already knew Sir Thomas wasn't in the mummy room. He wasn't in the coffin room. I didn't look too closely at the dark shadows in the kitchen, but I felt pretty sure he wasn't in there, either.

"Let's check out the wax museum."

"No way!" Carly hates the wax museum. She squinched up her eyes. "Anywhere but the wax museum!"

"All right." I paused and thought about where a ghost might be lurking. "How about the conservatory?"

Before Carly could think of some dumb excuse, I led her toward the back of the house.

When we first moved into the house on Fear Street, it took me a long time to figure out what a conservato-

34

ry was. Dad finally explained that it was a sort of greenhouse. The huge, empty, roller rink–size room had a glass ceiling and glass walls on one end. The original owners of the house used to grow all kinds of plants in there, even in the winter.

Dad hardly ever used the conservatory for museum exhibits. It was way too big. And really needed some repairs.

We pushed open the door and went inside. Eerie blue moonlight shone down through the glass walls and domed roof.

We crept along, close to the wall, and then ducked under the tropical plants Dad planned to use in the mummy exhibit. I peered through the big, floppy leaves. Something up ahead flashed and sparkled.

Like moonlight glinting off armor.

With one finger on my lips, I signaled Carly to keep quiet. We tiptoed through the shadows side by side. A cobweb trailed across my face. I brushed the sticky web aside. And caught my breath.

Sir Thomas! There he was.

He sat on a full-size model horse, right in the middle of the conservatory. The high glass dome arched above him.

I blinked.

For a second I thought I saw him move.

I blinked again.

I took a step closer.

"Awesome!" My voice echoed in the big empty room.

A high ladder stood next to the model horse. The ladder Dad always used to set up his exhibits.

"See? You were scared for nothing." I knew I didn't have to whisper anymore. "Dad and Mr. Spellman must have done it. They must have moved the knight in here when we were doing our homework."

I noticed then that they had also moved most of Dad's medieval weapons in here, too. Almost his entire collection. About a dozen lances hung on the wall to the left of the knight. And on the wall to the right of the knight I saw a display of big metal swords and shields.

Propped up in the corner, I spotted Dad's fake suit of armor, too. He'd bought it for a display in the museum and it had all the details of real armor. It even looked real from a distance. But close up you could tell it was made of cheap, thin tin.

I'd always loved that fake armor. But now that we had the real thing, it didn't look like much.

"Looks like they brought a lot of stuff in here," I said.

Carly wrinkled her nose. "Why?"

"Why?" A Carly question if I ever heard one. "Probably because there's more room in here. More people will have a chance to see the armor and all the cool weapons a knight like Sir Thomas needed to fight his enemies."

I stared up at Sir Thomas again. "He's awesome, isn't he?"

"Yeah, awesome," she echoed halfheartedly.

Seated on the horse, Sir Thomas appeared ready to fight. He carried a long, pointy lance in one hand. His other hand wrapped around the horse's reins. In that same hand he also grasped a shield.

The ghostly white moonlight flickered off Sir Thomas's helmet. It sparkled against his lance. It made the armor glow with a powerful green light. Glow from the inside.

It was the coolest thing I ever saw in my whole, entire life. I wanted to get as close as I could. Really, really close.

I walked toward him.

"Mike, what are you doing?"

Over my shoulder I saw Carly take a step back. "Dad might not like it if you—"

"Dad won't mind."

Oh, yes, he would, a little voice inside said. *He'd mind big-time. You'll be grounded for the rest of your life if he catches you messing around with that armor.*

But I'm not going to mess with it, I answered the voice. *I only want a closer look. Just one tiny peek. I've got to see where that green glow is coming from. Dad will understand.*

"It's truly excellent, isn't it?"

I don't know if Carly answered me or not. I wasn't listening.

All of a sudden I had to touch the armor.

I stood really close now. I stretched up as far as I could. That didn't help much. Sir Thomas sat on his horse. And the horse stood on a platform. Like I said, I'm sort of short.

Hey, but that's what ladders are made for, right? I grabbed the ladder and started climbing up.

"Mike, you're not going to—"

I ignored Carly. I ignored everything. Everything but the weird feeling that traveled down my arms. Tingling in my fingers.

I climbed to the very top of the ladder.

From up there the armor looked better than ever. I caught my breath. I studied the fancy designs on the breastplate and helmet. There were even a couple dents. I figured Sir Thomas got those in battle.

I gazed at the visor. The part the knight raised so he could eat and talk.

I gazed into the slit above the visor. The space where the knight looked out. It looked dark and empty.

I hooked my left arm around one side of the ladder. Then I leaned out as far as I could. My fingers brushed Sir Thomas's helmet.

The tingling got stronger.

"See. Nothing to worry about." I glanced down. Carly stared up at me. Her eyes were round. Her mouth hung open. "I bet I can even get a look inside."

Stretching out really far, I hooked my finger around the bottom of Sir Thomas's visor. I nudged it open.

The visor squeaked.

It didn't squeak like the museum floor squeaked. That was a friendly kind of squeak.

This squeak made my bones vibrate. It made my teeth ache.

The ladder wobbled. I steadied myself.

Before I even realized it, I stood face-to-face with the helmet.

Nothing to see. Nothing but a blackness. Blacker than the night.

I leaned over farther and peered inside. Blackness. Thick, dense.

I caught a whiff of something putrid—a pile of old garbage that had been around awhile. Say, a few centuries.

I felt sick to my stomach.

Then I heard a long groan. Like someone moaning from the other end of a long tunnel.

The sound grew louder. It filled my head. It drowned out the noisy *whoosh* of the blood rushing in my ears.

I leaned back and felt the ladder wobble under me. My entire body broke out in gooseflesh.

Something was moving. Inside the helmet. Something was coming. A black shadow!

The shrieking and moaning grew louder. And louder.

The armor trembled. Then shook violently.

With a ghastly cry that chilled my bones, the shadow rose up out of the armor.

I was done for.

6

The shadow rose out of the armor and came straight at me.

With my eyes squeezed shut, I heard a creepy sound of fleshy wings flapping around my head and neck.

I swatted wildly at the air. Then it flew around my head and dived at me from the other side.

I tried to duck. Too late.

The biggest, blackest, ugliest bat that ever lived flew right into my face.

I stared into two terrifying glowing red eyes. The bat's horrid mouth opened, baring sharp fangs. I saw its wicked claws flex. Ready—ready to dig into me.

I swung my arms over my head as the bat swooped at me again. Big, creepy wings flapped against my ear.

"Whoa!" I yelped. I lost my balance and fell backward off the ladder.

I landed on the floor with a thud. I felt like a bug hitting a car windshield.

"Are you all right?" I looked up and saw Carly standing over me. She offered me a hand up.

With a loud grunt I pulled myself to my feet. All my bones seemed to be in one piece. But just barely. I'd lost one of my slippers, and my pajamas had twisted all around my legs.

"Have a nice flight?" Carly asked sweetly.

"Very funny." I dusted off the seat of my pajamas. I spotted my missing slipper over by Sir Thomas's horse. I grabbed it and slipped it on. "That bat had to weigh at least fifty pounds. Its wings stretched out about a yard."

Carly made a face. "Bats! Yuck! Where did it go? Is it still here?" She covered her head and stared at the ceiling.

"I don't know," I said. "It just flew away."

Carly glanced at the ceiling again. "I don't know about you, but I'm going back to bed."

"Go ahead." I stepped back to let her by.

I watched Carly quickly walk out of the conservatory. She disappeared into the shadows on the far side of the room. A minute later I heard the sounds of her footsteps as she climbed the stairs.

I sighed. It was late. I had school tomorrow. First thing in the morning I had to give my report. I hoped I didn't nod out right in the middle of it.

Staying up suddenly seemed like a huge waste of time.

Had I found a ghost?

No.

All I found was my stupid sister.

And a bat.

I sighed. Pretty disappointing. I headed for the door. My slippers scuffed across the floor.

But about halfway across the room I thought I saw something. Out of the corner of my eye.

Something moving.

Metal flashing in the moonlight.

I stopped and squinted through the shadows at the armor.

Wasn't Sir Thomas staring in the *other* direction the last time I looked at him?

I shook my head. I rubbed my eyes.

No. Couldn't be.

Right?

The question tapped at my brain. My insides suddenly quivered. I decided to get out of the conservatory. Fast.

My racing footsteps slapped against the tile floor.

My heart pounded against my ribs.

At the door I quickly glanced back at Sir Thomas. He was right where he belonged.

I let out a deep breath and started the long trek to the stairs.

I crept through the kitchen, finding my way by the light of the moon. A cold, spooky glow flowed through the windows.

The moonlight shimmered against a huge, old broadsword hanging on the wall. Next to the sword hung a set of heavy chains. The links looked like teeth.

Hungry teeth. Grinning at me.

I couldn't help it. I shivered.

Get a grip, I told myself. You're acting like a dweeb. A total nerd. This is the Museum of History's Mysteries, right? It's home, right? What are you scared of?

I didn't stop to answer myself. I just walked a little faster.

The coffin room looked exactly the way we had left it.

Or did it?

The lid on Dracula's coffin . . . I didn't remember it being open like that. Just a tiny crack.

I didn't stop to check it out. I dashed into the mummy room.

44

I saw good old Charlie. Right where he always stood. His eyes still stared their mummy stare. His arms still jutted out straight. Mummy fingers dangling.

Reaching for me as I rushed past.

A flutter in the pit of my stomach told me not to think about that.

But by then it was too late.

My head whirled. I took a deep breath.

And choked on a mouthful of mummy dust.

I needed fresh air. Fast.

I bolted out of the mummy room. Up ahead I saw the doors that led out of the museum. The doors in the parlor. I sprinted toward them, coughing and gasping.

Air. I needed air.

The doors are the big, double kind. The kind they have at school. They have those metal handles that you press down to open. I grabbed the door handle and pressed.

The door didn't move.

I tried again. I pushed against it with my whole body.

Nothing. The door didn't budge an inch.

I dragged my hand over the wall. I felt the light switch and flicked on the overhead lights. Something told me I wasn't going to like what I saw.

My breath caught in my throat. It was a knight's sword.

Someone had jammed it right through both sets of door handles.

I threw myself against the doors and pulled and pulled at the sword. It was heavy. It didn't budge.

I was trapped!

7

"Trapped."

I heard my voice echo in the emptiness all around me.

I stood up again and wrapped both my hands around the cold, hard handle of the sword. I took a deep breath and pulled again.

Harder and harder.

My arms ached and blood pounded in my head.

No use.

Panting, I beat the sword with my fists.

Nothing.

I backed up and gave the door and the sword a ninja kick.

My foot throbbed with pain. But the sword didn't even jiggle.

Trapped.

This time the word echoed inside my head.

I had to backtrack. Through the entire museum. Through the mummy room. The coffin room. And the creepy kitchen.

I had to go through the conservatory. I had to reach the back door at the far side of that room. Or else . . .

I stopped myself from thinking that far. I didn't want to think about the evil knight. Not now.

"I can't be trapped. I can't be trapped. I can't be trapped."

I chanted the words out loud as I ran through the dark shadowy rooms.

"How could I be trapped? Carly went out that way. Just a couple minutes ago. There's no way anyone could have stuck that sword in the door since then. I would have seen them. Sure. Yeah. That's right. No way. I would have seen them for sure."

I kept walking and talking out loud to myself. And I hung on to my blue marble pendant. I'm not sure why. But I felt better when I was holding it. Braver.

I stopped at the conservatory door. I opened it a crack and peeked inside.

Sir Thomas was still there—sitting on his horse.

Just like when I left him.

I didn't breathe a sigh of relief. I don't think I

breathed at all. The whole time. I held my breath as I brushed under Dad's weird plants. I held my breath as I hurried past the ladder.

When I got all the way past Sir Thomas and nothing happened, I finally let the breath go. I didn't slow down, but the knots in my stomach loosened up a little.

The back door loomed closer. And closer. I walked faster. And faster. It came closer still.

Almost in reach now.

Then I heard a strange sound.

A creaking sound.

Shivers raced up my arms and legs. My knees wobbled.

I told myself, "Keep walking. Do *not* turn around and look."

The creaking grew louder.

But I had to look. I couldn't stop myself.

I turned very slowly.

What I saw made me freeze in place. My heart stopped.

The suit of armor.

Standing right behind me. Towering over me.

How did it get off the horse?

I took a gulp of air and forced myself to look up.

Through the slit above the visor I saw a fiery red glow. When my gaze met that glow, it grew brighter. Hotter. Redder.

Then I knew.

Sir Thomas. He was in there.

The armor creaked as he took a step closer.

I felt myself stumbling backward. The room spun.

"I . . . I . . . I . . ." I sputtered, trying to stay on my feet. Never taking my gaze off him for a second.

Then with the scraping sound of metal against metal, Sir Thomas raised one hand. He pointed right at me.

I stopped sputtering. My mouth hung open.

"You!" His deep voice boomed from inside the suit of armor. "You will not escape me this time, evil wizard!"

8

"**M**e? A wizard?" I choked out the words.

"Wait a second," I sputtered. "I'm just a sixth grader at Shadyside Middle School. Ask anybody. I'm no wizard."

"Save your wizard's lies for fools!" Sir Thomas's words boomed all around me.

The glass dome above us rattled and groaned, as if blasted by a huge gust of wind.

"It is your doing, wicked one. You and your magic trapped me in this metal tomb with your evil magic."

"Me?" I shook from head to toe. My pendant swung back and forth across my chest. The blue smoke inside it swirled.

"You've got me mixed up with somebody else. Honest. I've never even seen you before today, Sir Thomas. Sir Thomas, sir, I mean—" I added. Grownups usually like it when you act all polite. I figured it was worth a try.

No such luck.

"Vile one!" he roared. The fire behind Sir Thomas's visor grew bloodred and flickered. He tilted his head to take a closer look at me.

The next second I heard a furious snarl. Moving way faster than a guy should have been able to move wearing a couple hundred pounds of armor, Sir Thomas raised his lance. He lunged at me. He held the point of it right at my throat. "Prepare to die, hateful wizard!"

The needle-sharp lance pricked my skin. The metal felt fiery hot.

He wanted to kill me.

Slice me in half.

Chop me up in little pieces. And then even smaller pieces after that.

I didn't stand a chance against him.

I swallowed hard and took a giant step back.

Sir Thomas rattled forward. He snarled again. The flames behind his visor flickered and hissed.

"Did you think you could fool me by taking the shape of a young boy?" Sir Thomas roared at me. "I fought you when you turned yourself into a dragon. I fought you when you changed yourself into a wall of fire. And now . . ."

The knight dug the lance tip into my skin. "Now, wizard, I will have my revenge!"

I tried to scream for help. I tried to scream for Dad. Or even Carly.

I croaked pathetically.

Sir Thomas dipped his head and made a deep metallic grinding sound.

I took a couple of steps back.

The knight took a couple steps forward. He tossed his lance away. It clattered to the floor.

Great! He finally believes me, I thought.

Then he stepped even closer.

"I have waited centuries for this moment, wizard. I want to see your evil eyes as you gasp for your dying breath," his deep voice bellowed.

I stared up at him, frozen with fear. I couldn't move. I backed toward a corner. No place to hide. And I knew I'd never get past him alive.

Dad had set up a whole bunch of medieval weapons around the horse. Too bad for me. Sir Thomas had his pick.

"Should I use the broadsword?" Sir Thomas grabbed for it. "Or the mace?" He picked up the mace in his other hand.

He swiped the big, heavy sword through the air. In the moonlight the sharp blade gave off an icy glint.

Then he held out the mace at arm's length.

Sir Thomas's mace looked like a big club. Studded with spikes all around the top. Metal spikes filed to needle-sharp points.

They sparked at me. They flashed.

I cringed. I imagined what they would feel like biting into my skin.

"Chivalry!" I screamed the word. I forced myself to sound brave.

"You call yourself a knight? A real knight wouldn't attack an unarmed person. A real knight wouldn't go against the code of chivalry. Mr. Spellman said so."

The red glow behind the visor flickered.

"You are correct, foul wizard," Sir Thomas admitted. "I cannot attack an unarmed man." He stepped back and swept his arm out over Dad's display of weapons. "Choose."

My hands shaking, my heart pumping, I looked over the weapons. Could I save myself with any of them? Not likely. I picked up a heavy shield. One big enough to hide behind. I clutched it in both hands and ducked in back of it.

Great, I thought.

But not good enough for Sir Thomas.

"Choose!" he roared again.

His command made the conservatory windows rattle.

54

I dodged out from behind the shield long enough to grab the handle of a mace.

I held the shield in my left hand. I balanced the mace in my right. They weighed about a ton each and my arms ached just trying to hold on to them. How could I ever fight?

Would I even get a chance to try?

Sir Thomas threw his head back and laughed.

The battle had begun.

Lucky for me, I'm fast when I have to be. Even in reverse. My feet skidded on the tile floor as I slid backward. I peered over the top of the shield. I saw Sir Thomas pull his mace back, over his head. Then swing it toward me.

The pointy spikes glistened as the mace streaked through the air. I yelped and pushed the shield up in front of me. I ducked my head and braced myself.

Direct hit.

My bones shook as the mace crashed into my shield. A shower of sparks flew off the shield.

And then I heard a horrible cracking sound.

I knew it meant only one thing.

My crumbling shield wouldn't last much longer.

I squeezed my eyes shut.

Sir Thomas had won.

9

I held my breath. I counted my pounding heartbeats. I knew they'd be my last.

In two seconds I'd be face-to-face with the evil knight. With no shield to protect me.

One. Two. Two and a half.

Two and three-quarters . . .

Nothing happened.

I opened one eye. I opened my other eye.

I checked out my shield. Not a crack in sight.

I spotted Sir Thomas a few steps in front of me. He stared down at his mace.

I stared at it, too.

What remained of it.

When it struck my shield, Sir Thomas's mace

shattered into about a million little pieces. The sharp metal spikes scattered all over the floor.

While Sir Thomas looked closer at the ruined weapon, I peered at the front of my shield. The mace had made a big dent in it, all right. But nothing more.

"Wow!" I couldn't believe my luck.

What was going on here?

Sir Thomas snarled. The red glow behind his visor flared. He hurled his useless mace into the corner. "Wow?" he mimicked. "Do not try your magic words on me, vile creature!"

I spotted his broadsword, gripped in his other metal hand. He sliced the air with some practice swipes as he stomped toward me. The long silver blade flashed in the darkness.

I ducked down and ran for it.

Go! Go! Go! I urged myself.

I couldn't get out the conservatory door. Sir Thomas was blocking it. I pounded through the conservatory. Toward the kitchen. Sir Thomas pounded the floor one step behind me. I threw down the heavy shield. My legs pumped until every muscle ached. My breath burned in my throat.

I heard him close behind me. Closing the small gap. I imagined him reaching out a long metal arm and snagging me by the neck.

I ran even harder.

I punched the door open and raced into the kitchen. My slippers skidded on the tile floor. My feet flew out from under me.

I flailed my arms, trying to keep my balance. Too late. With a painful thud, I landed on my belly and kept sliding.

I heard Sir Thomas's sword whiz through the air above me.

Right where my head would have been.

Our kitchen has one of those islands in it. The kind of counter that stands in the middle of the floor. Regular people use it to cook and serve food. Dad uses it for cleaning weapons.

Scuttling like a beetle, I crawled behind the island. I hopped to my feet and darted to the other end of it, just beyond Sir Thomas's reach.

From my side of the counter I stared over at the knight. The space behind Sir Thomas's visor glowed with bloodred fire. Angry orange sparks shot out from the center of the crackling flames.

What could I use to fight him? I frantically scanned the room. The chains hanging on the wall? Too far away. The broadsword hanging beside them? Too heavy for me even to lift.

Then I saw it.

The catapult.

It stood between me and the door. I could dart over to it and take cover before I dived for the door.

If I could make my feet move.

Fear rooted me to the floor. I felt numb. Paralyzed.

Sir Thomas knew it. The fire in his eyes blazed. He raised his broadsword and whacked it down.

I darted out of the blade's path. Just in time.

The huge blade sliced clean through the countertop.

I crouched behind the catapult and gasped for breath.

With a growl Sir Thomas yanked his sword out of the counter. He swung it from side to side.

With his armor creaking and rattling, he marched toward me.

I could either die here behind the catapult or make one last, desperate dash for the door.

I spun around, all set to go for it.

My hand hit the lever that operated the catapult.

I heard a *boing*ing sound and a *whoosh*. Dad kept a papier-mâché rock in the catapult. I watched it sail toward the knight. I knew it couldn't hurt him, but maybe it would distract him long enough for me to sneak out the door.

It struck him square in the chest.

I dashed to the door. But out of the corner of my eye I saw Sir Thomas stagger back. His arms flew up from his sides. His broadsword and shield clattered to the floor.

The knight raised his head. He looked right at me. The fire in his eyes exploded like lava in a volcano.

Then he fell back onto the floor with a terrible crash.

Knocked out cold.

10

Knocked out? From a papier-mâché rock?

No way.

I came out from behind the catapult really slowly. I stared down at him.

His motionless legs and one arm stuck out from his body at weird angles. His other arm had dropped near the door.

His helmet was tilted to one side. I peered into the slit above his visor but saw only a cold black shadow.

Right in the middle of his breastplate I saw a huge dent.

The knots in my stomach untied. I dragged in a deep breath. It felt like the first one I'd taken in hours.

I spotted the rock under the kitchen table and picked it up. Light as a feather. As always.

A papier-mâché rock couldn't knock out a knight in heavy armor.

But it did!

And I beat the ghastly ghost!

"Yes! Way to go!" I cheered out loud for myself.

"He's lean. He's mean. He's Mike Conway! Undefeated champion—" I announced in my sportscaster's voice.

"Mike?" Dad called from the hallway. He came into the kitchen with Carly. "What's going on down here? Why aren't you in bed?"

Before I could get a word out, Dad flipped on the light.

He gasped. His face turned white. He stared down at the mess of armor on the floor. His mouth hung open.

Then he looked at me.

What a look!

Sir Thomas hadn't killed me. But it looked as if Dad wanted to. Real bad, too.

"Michael Conway! Didn't I tell you to keep your hands off that armor?"

"Now, wait a second, Dad. It's not what you think—"

"It was the bats," Carly piped up. She had on her I-told-you-so face. She crossed her arms over her chest.

"I told you about the bats, Dad. Mike was so afraid of them, he probably ran all over the place, knocking everything over. Including the armor."

"Shut up, Carly. What do you know?" I said. "It was Sir Thomas, Dad," I tried to explain. "He was chasing me all over the place. He called me a wizard. He tried to smash me with his mace, and then he chased me with his sword—" I was speed talking, but I couldn't stop. I wasn't even sure if Dad understood a word I was saying.

"And then, he—"

Suddenly Dad didn't look so sleepy anymore. Behind his glasses, his eyes opened wide.

"The knight? It was him?" Dad grabbed my shoulders. I stopped talking and took a breath. "He made that racket?"

I nodded wildly. Finally he heard me.

"That's wonderful!" Dad said.

"No, Dad. You don't understand."

"You mean he's really haunted?" He stared down at Sir Thomas again. He scooped up the arm that had fallen near the door. He waved it in the air. "What news! What wonderful news! Kids, do you know what this means?"

I darted in front of him. He still didn't understand!

"Dad, listen. The armor's not just haunted. It's dangerous. The knight tried to chop me into a million pieces. He tried to—"

I might as well have told the story to the wall.

Dad didn't hear a word I said. I had never seen him so excited.

"This is great! Better than great! The armor really is haunted. Carly. Mike." He turned to us. "You're looking at the most brilliant man on Fear Street. We'll make a mint. We'll . . ."

He went on and on like that. The more he went on, the lower my shoulders sagged.

"Did he really come down off his horse by himself, Mike?" he asked me. "Did he walk? Did he say anything?"

"Yes, he walked! Yes, he talked!" I yelled at Dad. "And then he tried to slice me in half with a huge sword!"

I never yelled at Dad. We weren't allowed. But this was an emergency.

If he would only listen for two seconds.

I snatched the sleeve of his gray robe.

"Dad, the ghost is here—now. The curse is on us. Whoever owns the armor is doomed. You've got to believe me!"

Dad laughed. He still didn't get it. Or maybe he thought I was acting so crazy because I'd seen a ghost.

His eyes glittered. He rubbed his hands together. "We can add an addition next spring. We'll have to, there will be so many customers."

"But, Dad. Dad, I—"

Dad slipped one arm around my shoulders. He grabbed Carly with the other one. He pressed us both into a huge hug. "We did it!" he said. "We saved the museum! Thanks to Uncle Basil, we've got our very own ghost."

Dad nudged us toward the stairs in the living room. "Well," he said, "I think that's enough excitement for one night. Or should I say one k-n-i-g-h-t?" He laughed at his own joke.

I didn't.

My heart sank. So did my hopes of making Dad listen.

He flicked off the kitchen light. He led us out of the museum. Dad and Carly headed up the steps. He kept talking a mile a minute. "The media, that's what we need. I'll call the TV stations in the morning. And the newspapers. We'll set up a grand opening. A grand unveiling of the haunted knight! This summer the tourists will be waiting in a line a mile long."

Still chuckling, I heard Dad tell Carly good night. Then I heard the sound of his bedroom door closing gently behind him.

Left alone, I kicked at the bottom step. Now what? I had to do something. But I couldn't figure out what.

It was no use.

I was too tired.

And too worried.

There was nothing to do but head back to bed.

I stood at the top of the steps when I thought I heard something. Something that didn't sound right.

I listened hard.

I heard it again. Louder this time.

The short hairs on the back of my neck stood up on end.

I recognized the sound.

The ghostly *clip-clop* of a horse's hooves.

The next day I rushed straight home after school. I dumped my backpack in the upstairs kitchen and grabbed some cookies. Then I ran into the museum, looking for Mr. Spellman.

Dad wouldn't listen to me. But I knew Mr. Spellman would.

I found him in the conservatory working on Sir Thomas. I saw the armor in one piece again stretched out flat on the floor next to the horse. Mr. Spellman was polishing the knight's broadsword.

He turned and smiled when I ran in. "Home from school already, Mike?" he said.

"Mr. Spellman, there you are. Dad wouldn't listen to me last night. But maybe you can warn him."

Mr. Spellman's bushy eyebrows shot up. "Warn him? About what?"

"The armor! It's haunted. Just like the story you told me," I gasped.

"That's what your dad said." He nodded. "He's making big plans for the grand opening next weekend."

"Oh, no!" I collapsed onto the floor. I shook my head. "I hope it's not too late," I said.

"Too late for what? What's wrong, pal?" Mr. Spellman sat down on the floor next to me. His old knees creaked.

I drew in a deep breath. Finally someone would listen to me. Everyone would be safe from Sir Thomas.

Even if it did ruin Dad's grand opening.

Sitting there on the floor, I told Mr. Spellman the whole story, start to finish. His blue eyes widened as he listened. He nodded a few times. But he didn't interrupt me once.

When I finished, Mr. Spellman didn't make fun of me, like Carly did. He didn't get all excited, like Dad did.

He just nodded his white head again. He pulled on his mustache. He was thinking really hard. After a little while he hoisted himself to his feet. He offered me a hand up.

"Mike, you should be proud of yourself," Mr.

Spellman said. "You fought the knight. You beat him. You broke the curse!"

"Do you really think so?" I asked. "But what if Sir Thomas comes back? What if I didn't break the curse? What if he's just waiting for the right time?"

"Hmmm." Mr. Spellman tugged on his mustache again. "I don't know, Mike. It sounds as if you put his evil spirit to rest for once and for all." Mr. Spellman glanced over at the armor. "He looks pretty harmless now, doesn't he?"

I looked at the armor, too. Last night, lit from within with Sir Thomas's ghostly red fire, it had terrified me. Right now in the sunlight the armor did seem harmless.

Maybe Mr. Spellman was right. Maybe I had defeated the knight for good.

But then I remembered Dad's big plans.

All the reporters. All the tourists.

Everyone expected a ghost.

"But what about Dad's big plans? No ghost, no grand opening."

"Yes, you've got a point there." He scratched his head. "Too bad your dad has invited every reporter in town."

"Every reporter?" I echoed.

"TV, radio, newspapers. The works." Mr. Spellman nodded. "He'll be crushed if there's no ghost." He sighed.

I sighed, too.

"Yeah, he'll be crushed," I said.

Mr. Spellman turned to me slowly. "Maybe we shouldn't tell him."

"We shouldn't?"

"Well, when you think about it, what good will it do? No one can guarantee when a ghost will show up anyway. Let the reporters come." He smiled. "The museum could use the publicity, right?"

"I guess so. That makes sense."

"Why upset your dad and ruin his plans?" Mr. Spellman continued in a low voice. He glanced at the armor again. "And who knows—Sir Thomas might return just to be on the five o'clock news."

I grinned. "That would really be something."

"Sure would." Mr. Spellman smiled back.

"I guess you're right," I said. "We won't tell Dad."

"We won't tell anyone," Mr. Spellman agreed.

I nodded. "But I'll keep an eye on Sir Thomas."

"Me, too." Mr. Spellman patted my shoulder. "Now I must get back to work. Want to help put Sir Thomas on his horse?"

I stood up and gazed over at the armor. I put my hands in my pockets.

"Uh—well, I really want to—" I stammered. "But I need to study for this huge math test."

Mr. Spellman chuckled. "Sure thing, Mike. Maybe next time."

He smiled and winked at me.

* * *

70

That night I couldn't sleep. I leaned back against my pillows and gazed into the blue pendant. And worried.

I worried that Sir Thomas *would* return. He'd charge through the museum and make confetti out of all of us.

Then I worried that the ghost was gone and Dad's grand opening would be a flop. And the thought almost made me wish the ghost would return.

I worried so much that I almost didn't hear it.

Thump. Thump.

I sat up. I listened.

Thump. Thump.

"Very funny, Carly." Grumbling, I got out of bed. "How dumb do you think I am?"

I went downstairs. The sounds grew louder. I followed them. Right back to the kitchen.

"The kitchen? Again?" I shook my head in amazement. Carly didn't have much of an imagination.

Without bothering to turn on the lights, I walked through the museum and into the kitchen.

Thump. Thump.

I heard it, louder than ever. But I didn't see Carly. Anywhere.

For a couple of seconds I stood stone still. I didn't take a breath. I didn't move a muscle.

Until somebody grabbed my arm.

71

I shrieked and jumped out of my slippers.

"Sorry, Mike."

Mr. Spellman! As soon as I saw him, I relaxed. But not for long.

Something was up.

Mr. Spellman put one finger up to his lips. "I didn't mean to scare you," he whispered. "I was working late in the mummy room when I heard the sound. What do you suppose it is?"

I shrugged. "Probably Carly. She has a rotten sense of humor."

Mr. Spellman crept over to the door of the conservatory. He peeked inside. "It sounds as if it's coming from in here. What do you say? Should we investigate?"

I swallowed hard. My tongue felt thick. My mouth felt dry.

"But, Mr. Spellman," I began, "what if—"

Mr. Spellman didn't let me finish. He gave me a reassuring smile. "Don't worry, Mike. We'll be really careful. I believe you about the haunted armor. I'm not going to take any chances. Not with a ghost as evil as Sir Thomas. Nothing will happen to you. I promise."

I'm not a chicken. But I know one thing. I never would have had the nerve to check out that noise without Mr. Spellman. I followed him into the conservatory.

The second we set foot inside the door, the thumping noise stopped.

Mr. Spellman made sure I stayed in back of him. He led us over to the exhibit.

I spotted Sir Thomas up on his horse. His head facing forward. His lance held high.

Nothing looked out of place.

"Well, I guess we're both wrong this time." Mr. Spellman didn't whisper anymore. He looked as relieved as I felt. "It wasn't the ghost after all."

Mr. Spellman turned around to leave the room. I did, too.

I took one step. Then something whizzed by my head. Close enough to skim my hair.

I saw Mr. Spellman's face turn white.

Then I heard something explode.

A long, thick arrow had slammed into one of Dad's flowerpots not ten feet away. The arrow stuck up from a pile of dirt and the jagged remains of the pot. I knew right away what kind of arrow it was.

It was an arrow from a crossbow.

A knight's crossbow.

Mr. Spellman and I turned around at the same moment.

Just in time to see Sir Thomas charge.

12

"**R**un for it!" I yelled at Mr. Spellman as I took off at top speed.

I headed for the door. I heard the horse's hooves pounding behind me. Getting louder. Coming closer. Closing the gap between us.

I darted to my right and the knight followed. I veered off to the left. He pulled hard on the horse's reins and stayed right behind me.

I glanced over my shoulder.

Mr. Spellman was beside me. And behind him was the knight.

The red fire behind Sir Thomas's visor was blinding. He held his lance high. I saw the sharp tip. Aimed right at me.

Up ahead the door seemed an impossible distance away.

I pushed myself harder. My lungs burned. I reached out desperately. The door still looked miles away.

Another second and the lance would be right through my back.

I heard a noise. A *whooshing* sound. Like rushing wind.

I braced myself for the blow.

Nothing happened.

I spun around. So scared that I grabbed Mr. Spellman's hand.

All the lances from Dad's exhibit came whizzing off the wall and over my head. Aimed right at the knight.

Some of the lances hit the floor right in front of Sir Thomas and stuck there. Some of them stuck in the floor in back of him. Lances stuck up from the floor to the knight's right. They stuck up to his left.

A cage of lances surrounded him. The knight was trapped. His horse snorted. It stomped the ground.

Sir Thomas let out a deafening roar. He waved his arms over his head. The red flames behind his visor shimmered.

"Wow!" I was flabbergasted. And relieved. I let go of Mr. Spellman. I took a chance and went over to the lances to check them out.

How did this happen? I couldn't figure it out.

That's when I noticed my pendant.

The blue smoke inside the marble swirled and bubbled. Glimmering with a weird blue light. Brighter than Sir Thomas's spooky eyes.

"Wow!" I know, I should have been able to come up with something better to say, but "Wow" seemed to cover all the bases.

It had to be the pendant. It was magic!

Now it had saved me for a second time.

What else could make a papier-mâché rock destroy a suit of armor? What else could make a row of lances fly through the air?

"That's it! That's it, Mr. Spellman. Don't you get it?" I held the pendant up to the moonlight. "You were right! The first time you saw it you knew. The pendant! It *is* magic!"

Still holding the pendant up, I stepped closer to the knight.

Mr. Spellman stood behind me. This time the swords Dad had hung on the wall for display clattered against each other. Battle-axes streaked by in the air.

Awesome!

I could hardly believe it. I tested some more. Waving the pendant, I moved toward the knight.

Sir Thomas winced. He held one metal hand up in front of his face. The red fire behind the visor flickered and faded out.

"Hear me, wicked knight. I *am* a wizard!" I tried to

make my voice low and booming. The way I thought a wizard would sound.

Loud. Important. Powerful.

"I command you to stop attacking us!"

I jabbed the pendant in Sir Thomas's direction.

The swords crashed and smashed over the knight's head. He waved his arms at them. They kept crashing and smashing.

I lifted the pendant up. The round glass orb caught the moonlight. It sparkled. Then it shot a dazzling beam of blue light at Sir Thomas.

As the light struck him, Sir Thomas sat bolt upright.

His armor shimmied and rattled for a second. And then . . .

Boom!

13

His helmet exploded off his shoulders and flew straight up to the ceiling.

A gust of red fire shot up out of the armor.

And then the whole thing fell apart.

Sir Thomas's breastplate clattered to the floor.

His shield fell out of his hands.

And then his arms fell off.

The knight's metal leg guards tottered, then hit the ground.

An awful smell, like burning rubber, hung in the air.

The knight had turned into a pile of scrap metal.

A spooky cloud of red smoke floated above the whole mess.

I held my nose and took a step closer. I heard a soft hissing. Soft, like air leaking out of a tire. I looked down at the pile of armor.

He was gone all right. Gone for good this time.

"I did it! I did it! Way to go, Conway!" I had never been so excited in my whole, entire life. I did a little dance through the last wisps of smoke.

"I really *am* a wizard!"

Then I heard another voice. A strange and chilling one.

"You witless newt! You did nothing. Nothing! I did it all!"

I froze in my tracks. This voice really did sound like a wizard. It boomed through the conservatory. The windows rattled all around me. The floor shook under my feet. The whole place filled with a swirling icy wind that made me shiver.

I spun around, looking for the source of that frightening voice.

"Fool! Do you really believe you possess magic powers?" The voice was coming from Mr. Spellman? Could it be?

He laughed and frosty fingers raced up my spine.

He smiled at me in a way I'd never seen him smile before. A way I didn't like.

His teeth looked pointy and sharp. His skin pulled tight across his face. Like a skull.

Something about his creepy smile made me feel as

if I'd been kicked right in the stomach. I couldn't believe it. I stepped closer to my friend. "Mr. Spellman?"

Mr. Spellman waved his hands. The motion made the air ripple all around me. My skin suddenly felt clammy. I broke out in a cold sweat.

"Do not call me by that ridiculous name, boy!" Mr. Spellman roared. "I am Mardren, the greatest wizard of all time! And now, little bug, I am finished with you!"

Slowly Mr. Spellman raised both his hands. They were covered with golden rings shaped like snakes. The snakes had glowing red and purple jewel eyes that winked in the moonlight. He pointed right at me.

The snake rings came alive. They slithered around his fingers. The snakes grew bigger and bigger. They crawled around his wrists, hissing. Ugly black tongues flickered at me.

A snake head darted out at me. I saw its jaws stretch open and long curved fangs poised to strike.

I leaped back.

Mr. Spellman waved his hands again. The hissing golden snakes transformed into lightning bolts, flashing from his fingertips. The lightning crackled in the air all around me. So close, I felt the lightning's heat as it zipped by my head.

I ducked down. Almost too late.

I smelled burning hair and touched my head. A few strands on top felt hot and singed.

I couldn't believe it. Mr. Spellman. My friend. All this time he tricked me. He tricked everyone!

Crouched down in a corner, I watched as his body transformed.

His eyes glowed. Not red like the knight's. White. Cold. Icy. Hard.

The skin on his face shimmered, like a bowl of Jell-O. Then it turned a sickly yellow-green color that looked dry and leathery. The lines around his eyes and mouth grew deeper and his nose stretched out, long and beak-shaped.

His mustache grew out, too. Long and wild-looking. And his cheeks sprouted a beard. A white beard, all tangled and knotted, that flowed down to his waist.

He waved one hand above his head, and suddenly a long silver stick appeared in his hand.

Then he twirled around, swinging the stick around over his head.

One. Two. Three times.

He spun at top speed, spinning into a complete blur. A purple blur.

I blinked.

He stopped and stood before me. A long purple robe flowed around his body. Purple boots covered his feet and a tall, pointed purple hat balanced on his head.

Symbols that glowed with strange light covered his robe and hat. Silver moons. Golden stars. Strange shapes I'd never seen before.

I saw a big blue circle, too. With swirling blue lights inside.

"My pendant!" I stared at the symbol on Mr. Spellman's robe. I looked down at my pendant.

It softly glowed.

"Mike, Mike, Mike." Mr. Spellman . . . er, Mardren laughed. I felt a creepy, pins-and-needles tingle all over my body. "You really thought you did it all, didn't you?" Mardren shook his head. He smiled a scary smile. "You ridiculous worm! You have no magic power. The power is all mine. I merely used you to destroy my most deadly foe."

Mardren pointed his long silver stick. Right at the pile of armor. With the toe of one purple boot he kicked aside Sir Thomas's helmet. It rolled into the corner.

Mardren chuckled. "Once every hundred years, Sir Thomas and I must fight each other," he explained. "If I defeat him, his ghost is doomed. He must stay a prisoner inside his armor for another hundred years. If he defeats me . . ." Mardren shrugged.

"Well, that is not going to happen, is it? At least not for another hundred years. You took care of that for me."

A memory flashed through my head. I thought about what the knight told me. About fighting the wizard as a dragon. And as a wall of fire.

"You are correct!" Mardren could read my mind! He said out loud everything I was thinking. "Sir Thomas thought you were me. He thought I had taken on the shape of a small, weak boy. It is not what I had planned. Not exactly. But it worked. Why do you think a wizard of my skill and power would hang around in this shabby place?"

The wizard looked around the conservatory. His face puckered up. His nostrils flared.

"With my powers I knew Sir Thomas would arrive here sooner or later. I knew it even before your uncle Basil found the armor in Dreadbury Castle and sent it here. I had to wait for Sir Thomas. I had to fight him."

Mardren stared hungrily at my pendant. His tongue flickered over his cracked lips. He smiled.

A shiver crawled up my back.

"You snatched the pendant before I could, bothersome boy," Mardren said. "That day the armor was delivered you reached first for the magic orb. You touched it first and put it on. There is a spell that gives the pendant its power. After you touched it, I could not take it away from you. No one could. Not until Sir Thomas was destroyed. Now . . ."

A slow smile inched up the edges of Mardren's mustache. He looked down at the pieces of Sir Thomas scattered on the floor. His eyes glittered.

"You took care of that for me. And I never faced any danger. If anyone had to get killed . . ." Mardren shook out his robe. The moons and stars on it flashed at me. "You see what I mean? Everything is perfect now. . . ."

Mardren swung around. He pointed his staff toward me. A single bolt of lightning flashed from the end of it. It shot right at my chest.

The pendant flashed, as if it answered the call of Mardren's magic. It rose right up off my chest. It jerked toward Mardren. It tugged me closer to the wizard.

"You have something that belongs to me, toad." Mardren touched the golden chain with the tip of his staff. The chain snapped. When Mardren lifted his staff, the blue marble globe stuck to the top of it.

"Now I have the magic pendant," Mardren said. "And Sir Thomas can no longer stop me from using it. This magic orb will make me even more powerful." He glanced at the marble. His face lit up with an evil smile.

Mardren looked down at me. "I am afraid I must get rid of you. I cannot allow you to give away my little secret. Hmmm. What should I do?"

84

Mardren sucked on his shriveled lower lip, thinking. Thinking about getting rid of me.

I swallowed hard. I quietly slid back a step. Run for it, I urged myself.

"Not so fast, toad!" he boomed at me. Mardren's look froze me on the spot. His eyes lit up. "That's it! I know exactly what to do. I will turn you into a mouse. Just be careful! Don't get too close to the cat!"

I caught my breath. It burned my lungs. My hands trembled at my sides.

Mardren saw me shake. Chuckling, he waved his hands over my head. "Keep still, pesky boy! The words of power must be spoken three times." He cleared his throat. His voice rang through the room.

"With the moon over the house, change this boy into a mouse. With the moon over the house, change this boy into a mouse. With the moon over the house, change this boy—"

"Stop!" another voice shouted.

Mardren gasped in surprise.

The voice sounded from the deep shadows on the other side of the conservatory. A deep hollow voice. It echoed. It rumbled.

My heart thumping, I watched a shape materialize out of the shadows. Slowly it clomped forward. With each step I could see more of it.

Metal shoes.

A broad breastplate.

A helmet with an empty space behind the visor.

The knight raised one metal glove. He pointed right at Mardren. His voice boomed.

"Wizard! You will not win!"

14

Sir Thomas. Back again!

The knight lumbered out of the shadows. He took one shaky step forward. Then another.

I stared at the knight—and gasped.

It wasn't Sir Thomas.

One of dad's fake suits of armor had come alive!

"Wh-what's going on here?" I stuttered. Was the ghost of Sir Thomas in *there* now?

I stepped back as the knight clattered forward—his sights set on Mardren this time.

I shot a glance at Mardren. Then the knight. Which one should I run from? Which one?

Before I could move, the wizard's eyes flashed. He

shook his shoulders. He spread his arms. He started the words of another spell.

The knight stomped closer. He swung out at the wizard with his long metal arm.

He missed Mardren by a mile. But one of his heavy metal gloves smacked the pendant on top of Mardren's staff.

The big blue marble wobbled. It teetered. It tumbled from the top of the staff.

Mardren lunged for it, grabbing for the beautiful blue marble as it fell through the air.

The tips of his long, gnarled fingers brushed it.

It slipped past his fingers.

And crashed to the floor.

The glass shattered, and a deafening boom echoed through the room. Louder than a clap of thunder.

A brilliant blue light flashed—flashed so bright I had to cover my eyes.

Then I heard a strange fizzing sound.

The pendant had burst into a zillion pieces. And now some of the shards of glass zipped through the air. Zipped through the air like tiny shooting stars!

Then a cloud of blue smoke swirled up from the floor. Up from the center of the jagged bits of glass that remained there.

It was the most amazing thing I had ever seen.

The blue mist floated over the floor like the fog that

sometimes hovers over the Fear Street Cemetery. It curled around my legs. Everywhere it touched me I felt cold to the bone.

Then it gathered in a cloud around Mardren. It slowly rose up, up, up over his flowing robe.

"No! No!" Mardren screamed. He waved his arms frantically. Trying to wave away the smoke. But the smoke continued to billow.

He puffed up his cheeks and blew at it.

Then he kicked at it with his purple boots.

The blue smoke thinned—and Mardren fell to his knees. Searching. Searching the floor for something.

What? What is he looking for? I wondered, staring hard through the mist.

And that's when I saw it.

A tiny golden sword—glittering in the moonlight.

I blinked in amazement. It must have been hidden in the marble the whole time. Hidden by the swirling smoke.

Mardren grabbed for the sword at the same time I did.

I reached it first.

"Slow as a snail!" I cried.

I snatched up the sword. The moment my fingertips touched it, a jolt of electricity shot through my hand. Raced up my arm. Hit me square in the chest, hard. I staggered back.

My fingers tingled—as if hundreds of pins and needles were piercing them. I didn't care. I held the tiny sword tight in my fist.

Another jolt shot through my hand.

Sparks flew from my fist.

I gaped at my hand—as the tiny sword began to grow, right in the center of my palm.

It grew and grew. Longer. Thicker. Heavier.

It grew until it was the size of a real knight's sword.

I grabbed on to its handle. It fit perfectly in my grip.

I stretched out my arm and waved it. The blade caught the moonlight. It twinkled with the light of a hundred stars.

Then a *whooshing* sound rushed through my ears. And, out of nowhere, pieces of golden armor appeared in the air. Like magic, they snapped onto my body.

Golden shin guards clicked onto my knees to protect my legs. A golden breastplate snapped over my chest.

Golden gloves slipped over my hands. And golden metal sleeves sprang out from them, covering my arms.

"All right!" I whooped.

My voice sounded funny. Echoing inside the helmet that had suddenly appeared over my head.

Holding the golden sword high, I spun around and faced Mardren.

I thought the wizard looked mad before. But that must have been his "have a nice day" face.

Mardren tossed back his head. His lips curled into a sneer—revealing his long, pointed teeth. He let out an ugly snarl. Sparks of lightning crackled from his fingertips.

"So you think you can defeat me?" he howled. A heavy wind whipped through the room, nearly knocking me down. "Nothing can destroy my magic!" he roared.

Mardren spread his arms wide—and started to grow. Into a towering giant.

A huge bolt of lightning exploded from the tip of his staff.

The conservatory lit up with a blinding white light. It hurt my eyes, and I squeezed them shut.

The lightning bolt hung in the air. It sizzled. Cracked and snapped. I could feel its intense heat through my armor—the heavy golden metal singed my skin.

With a sweep of his arm Mardren sent the deadly hot bolt on its course.

On its course—straight at me.

15

I leaped in the air. Just in time.

The lightning streaked beneath me. Inches below my metal shoes.

I staggered back and landed in the arms of the knight.

"Don't give up, Mike." The knight whispered the words against my helmet.

"Carly?" I gasped. "Is that you, Carly?"

"Yes!" she whispered, peeking out of the space between the breastplate and the bottom of the helmet. All I could see were her beady little eyes.

"You distract him," I whispered. "I'll run up and take my best shot."

"I can't see what I'm doing in this soup can," she

said. She pushed me back on my feet. "You've got to fight him alone!"

Then she shoved me forward.

I shook from head to toe. My armor rattled. I lifted one heavy leg and raised my sword.

Mardren stood tall. He sneered a wicked sneer.

I stared into his eyes, about to strike.

Mardren stretched out his arms. He held up a silver stick and waved his arms. His purple robe billowed all around him.

I jumped back.

He tossed his head back and shrieked long and loud. The skin on his face shimmered again, stretching out in all directions. His arms stretched out, his hands turning into big scaly yellow claws. His legs stretched, too, and his body puffed up, like a huge purple blimp.

Cackling wickedly, he floated up from the floor and sailed above me.

I staggered back. My mouth hung open.

I saw his neck stretch out and his beaky nose grow into a long snout. He swooped up to the very top of the ceiling, spinning around in the shadows.

I held tightly to my sword, getting ready for . . . I didn't know what!

I squinted at his dark, twisting form, sailing above me. Then it swooped down. Coming in for a landing.

I crouched down and covered my head.

Flapping wings beat the air and something huge snarled and hissed.

I gulped and looked up again.

I stood face-to-face with a dragon.

A gigantic, hideous dragon with big purple wings.

All over its huge body purple scales oozed foul-smelling slime. Three big yellow eyes rolled around in its head. Two long black forked tongues curled out its mouth. Disgusting green saliva dripped everywhere. The gluey drops sizzled as they hit the floor. The tiles vaporized.

I took a step forward. I swung my sword with both hands wrapped around the handle.

The dragon twisted its ugly head back. The two tongues curled out at me. The dragon sucked in a deep breath. Then blew it out. A putrid cloud hit me. It smelled horrible.

The disgusting stink turned my stomach upside down. It burned my eyes. Inside my armor I gasped for air.

I saw the dragon's huge jaws gape open again. I jumped back and braced myself for the smell.

My eyes widened as I saw a long stream of fire spew out his mouth. The flames licked the toes of my armor boots. My feet were burning up.

"Hey!" I yelped. I hopped from foot to foot. The dragon drew in another deep breath. I readied myself for another huge flame.

"Oh, no, you don't!" I saw Carly running toward us with a fire extinguisher. Dad kept them all over the museum, just in case.

Carly had removed Dad's armor, and she moved just fast enough.

She leaned back and aimed at the dragon. She pulled the lever and fired.

With a *pop* and a *whoosh,* foamy white stuff flew all over the place. The plume of foam shot right down the dragon's throat. It cooled off my feet.

"Way to go, Carly!" I gave her a high five.

When I looked back at the dragon, I saw only Mardren again.

Foamy white gunk dripped off his beard. Globs of it clung to his hat and his purple robe.

His yellow face twisted with anger.

"I am through playing games!" Mardren tossed his staff up in the air. He snapped his fingers. The staff came down again and magically turned into a gleaming sword.

Mardren grabbed the sword. He charged.

"Mike, look out!" Carly screamed.

I pushed her out of the way and raised my sword.

I looked up and there was Mardren.

A sword's length away.

Mardren swung. I blocked his swing with my golden sword. The two blades crashed together.

Sparks flew everywhere. My arm vibrated. It felt as if it had been yanked right off my shoulder.

The next time Mardren came at me, I dodged his sword.

Mardren jabbed low. I jumped. As fast and as high as I could.

By the time Mardren backed off, he was breathing hard. I panted, too. We glared at each other. Beads of sweat ran down my face. Dripping into my eyes. My heart pounded against the suit of magical armor.

Struggling to catch my breath, I kept my eyes on the wizard.

He raised his sword. I saw his lips flicker. I heard him mumble.

Mumble another wicked magic spell.

Mardren raised his sword straight up toward the sky. Purple sparks burst out of the end of it.

The purple fire hit the glass ceiling. It rained down all around us. Just looking at it made me feel dizzy. And sleepy.

Not a good sign.

"Don't look at it. Don't look at it." I kept repeating the warning over and over inside my head.

But I couldn't help it.

Mardren's magic sparks glittered like jewels. The sparks hypnotized me.

"Don't fall asleep now!" I told myself. "You'll be finished!"

I kept blinking my eyes. My eyelids felt so heavy. They drooped, almost closed. I shook my head. My head felt heavy, too. Too heavy to hold up.

I felt my eyes close and my head drop against my chest.

My knees were weak. I staggered forward. My knees buckled.

"No, Mike! No!" Carly shouted at me. Her voice sounded as if it came from really far away. "Don't let him do it!"

I'm not sure how I did it, but I forced my eyes open. The purple sparks fell all around me. I didn't want to think about what would happen if they hit me.

With every last little bit of energy I had, I clasped the sword in two hands and raised my arms.

I propped my sword up on my shoulder. When the sparks got close enough, I batted them with the sword.

Line drives. Grounders. High flies to center field.

Some of the sparks sputtered and sizzled. Some of them bounced. They hit the ceiling and fell down again.

Right on top of Mardren.

"No!" the wizard shrieked. He gave a bloodcurdling scream.

The sparks hit his hat. I heard hissing. Each time one landed on him, I saw a puff of purple smoke rise. The sparks covered his purple robe. They landed all around him on the floor and burst into puffs of purple smoke.

The smoke got thicker. Darker. He tried to move away, but the smoky cloud clung to him. He couldn't shake it off.

In seconds he was standing in a thick, billowing purple cloud.

"No! No! You monstrous children! How could you do this to me?" Mardren waved his arms in the smoke.

Carly crept up beside me. Side by side, we watched the purple cloud cover Mardren from head to toe. And then close in on him.

"No! No!" Mardren's eyes bulged. His mouth twisted in a gruesome scowl.

I could hardly see him anymore. The weird symbols on his robe were dissolving in the smoke. Then his long white beard went up in smoke.

The smoke spread over his face. The cloud covered his eyes. The last thing to disappear was the very tip of the wizard's purple, pointy hat.

"No! No! No!" From out of the smoky cloud we heard Mardren's smothered voice. He whined and groaned. "This can't be happening. Not to me. You evil children! I am Mardren, the most powerful wizard in all the world. No! No . . ."

Mardren's voice got weaker and weaker. Finally I couldn't hear it anymore. The huge cloud of purple smoke swirled around. An awful smell made me choke and cough.

Except for my coughing, the place was suddenly as quiet as a tomb.

Carly and I stood there, listening. Waiting to see what would happen next.

From out of nowhere a cold wind swept through the conservatory. The purple cloud blew away.

Mardren had vanished completely in the smoke.

Or had he?

Right at the spot where the wizard had vanished, I saw something. A huge, hideous purple snail.

"Yuck!" Carly jerked back.

"He can't hurt us anymore." I went a little bit closer to the snail. Bulging red eyes dangled from the ends of long yellow antennae. Thick slime covered a big purple shell. A slimy snail body, a disgusting shade of green, wriggled beneath the shell.

I poked the snail with my golden sword. "Slow as a snail!" I said.

The snail's antennae wiggled in the air, and its eyes bugged out. It tossed its disgusting head. Then it slithered away.

All that was left of Mardren was a trail of purple slime.

16

"**M**ike, you were . . . you were . . ." Carly shook her head. Her smile grew wider and wider. "You were awesome!"

I whipped off my helmet. I couldn't help myself. I smiled, too.

"I *was* awesome, wasn't I?" I waved my sword over my head. I laughed.

"You were pretty awesome, too, Carly," I admitted. "What made you put on that armor?"

"I was going to play a joke on you," she admitted. "But then I heard what Mr. Spellman . . . er . . . Mardren . . . er . . . whoever he was . . . said! I knew Dad was out. I had no choice. There was no way I'd let him turn you into a mouse. I mean, what if the cat ate you? The poor thing would have gotten sick!"

"Thanks a lot!" I was too tired to think of anything funny to say. I'd get her later. After a few hours of sleep.

I yawned and tossed my sword down. The second I did, the rest of the golden armor unsnapped. The pieces clattered to the floor.

I sighed and wiggled my shoulders. I hadn't realized how heavy the armor felt.

"Boy, it's not easy being a knight in shining armor!"

I plunked down on the floor. Right next to the charred pile of Sir Thomas's armor. Now Dad would have to put it all back together again. I poked one of Sir Thomas's shoes with the tip of my sword. I pushed aside one of his gloves.

I set the golden sword down on the floor, between me and the pile of Sir Thomas's armor.

"I feel like I ran a couple miles," I said with a huge yawn. "I can't believe I—"

Something moved next to me. My words stuck in my throat. I heard Carly's muffled scream, but I didn't dare turn to look at her.

My gaze was stuck on Sir Thomas's glove.

All by itself the glove slid out of the pile and right over to the sword. One by one the metal fingers flexed. They closed around the handle of the golden sword.

"Yikes!" I rolled out of the way. I scrambled to my feet.

With the glove still holding on tight, the sword rose in the air. I heard a deep moan. The sound raised the hairs on the back of my neck. The moan started low. And sounded far away. But it got louder by the second. And closer.

Then it surrounded us.

The sword pointed toward the pieces of armor that protected Sir Thomas's legs. With a *whoosh* they rose up off the floor. They floated over to the sword and the glove. They stopped in the place where the knight's legs would be. Next, the sword pointed to the knight's metal boots.

"Mike!" Carly's fingers dug into my arm. "Mike, do something! He's coming back to get us!"

He was! I had to do something. Fast.

I made a diving grab for the boots.

The second my fingers touched the metal, I yelped and pulled them back. The armor stung my fingertips with cold.

I rubbed my hands to warm them. I saw the boots clatter away. Clanking against the tile floor, they marched into place right under the leg guards.

The moaning grew louder. It made my ears hurt. The breastplate flew into the air. It floated into place right above the knight's legs.

The arms came after that. With a clang they

snapped into place where the breastplate met the shoulders.

The other glove flew onto the arm that didn't have a hand. That hand gripped the golden sword, too.

I felt petrified. Worse than petrified. I could feel my pulse pounding against my temples. Hammering so hard, I felt my head about to explode.

Carly and I stared at Sir Thomas.

He stood before us in one piece again.

All except for his head.

With a piercing whistle that made the hair on my arms stand up on end, the sword swung and pointed at Sir Thomas's helmet.

With an answering wail that came from inside, the helmet slowly rose off the floor.

The helmet sailed past us. The air turned icy as it flew by.

The helmet glided over to the rest of the armor. With a click, it floated down into place.

The second it did, the fire behind the visor flared to life.

Sir Thomas's eyes flashed. They sparked. Not purple like Mardren's magical sparks.

Red.

Bloodred.

Sir Thomas didn't say a word. He lifted his sword.

He pressed the tip of it against my heart.

103

17

Sliced to ribbons.

We were about to be sliced to ribbons.

I watched the ugly fire in Sir Thomas's eyes flicker. He stepped forward and I felt the knife point jab me through my T-shirt.

I held my breath and waited to feel his sword run me through.

The knight turned his head. He looked at the puddle of smelly purple slime. Then he turned back and looked at me.

"Who has destroyed Mardren?" His question echoed from inside the armor.

I tried to answer him. But all that came out was a sputtering, choking sound.

Carly pushed me forward. "Mike did it," she said. "He turned the wizard's own magic against him."

The knight didn't move. I could feel his gaze burning from behind the visor.

"Is this true?" he asked.

"Yes," I croaked. "I didn't have much choice. First he tried to turn me into a mouse and then he shot purple sparks at me. But I batted them back at him. With that."

I pointed at the golden sword. My hand shook like crazy. "When the sparks hit Mardren, he was smothered in a cloud of purple smoke. Then he turned into a snail. A big, slimy purple one."

"A snail!" Sir Thomas boomed with laughter. His laugh had a deep metallic ring that echoed through the room. "A slimy purple snail! How fitting for the evil one!"

He laughed and laughed, and the red fire behind the visor settled down to a warm glow.

Suddenly he didn't seem nearly as scary. He didn't seem scary at all.

Sir Thomas knelt on one knee. He bowed his head. "Then, good sir, I owe you my thanks."

"What?" I looked down at his shining helmet. He still held his sword, but now it rested on the floor. "Is this some kind of trick? You mean you've stopped trying to chop me into little pieces?"

Sir Thomas shook his head. "You must forgive

105

me," he said. "When I saw you with the pendant, I thought you were Mardren. I thought the evil wizard had changed himself into a boy to deceive me. I see now that I was wrong. You were not in league with the wicked sorcerer." The knight looked around the museum. "All of you here, you were never my enemies. You were always my friends."

"Me?" I pointed at myself. A big, goofy smile lit up my face. "I'm your friend?"

"That is correct." Sir Thomas struggled to stand up. In spite of all the oil Dad had used on him, his joints were still pretty rusty. He creaked and wobbled.

I offered him a hand.

This time when I touched the metal, it didn't chill me to the bone.

"I know the story Mardren must have told you," the knight said once he came to his feet. "He told you I was evil. Am I right?"

I nodded.

"Mardren was a scoundrel. A vile and hateful creature." Sir Thomas raised his head. He held it high. "I was never evil. Mardren was the evil one. Many hundreds of years ago I fell in love with his beautiful daughter. He would not allow us to marry. He wanted her to have a husband who was richer and more powerful than I. He put a spell on me, trapping me forever in my suit of armor. I could only be free if

Mardren was defeated. And only one thing could defeat him—my golden sword."

Sir Thomas went over to the purple puddle. He touched it with the toe of his boot.

"But Mardren imprisoned my sword inside his magic pendant," he said. "Even though the pendant remained with me, I couldn't use it. I could never retrieve the sword inside. Without its power I grew weaker and weaker. I knew I'd never be able to fight the wizard. But you did it for me, Mike."

Sir Thomas laughed again. The sound made me feel warm. The way you feel laughing with a friend. "Because of your bravery, I will finally be free of this armor, which has been my prison and my tomb. But first . . ."

Sir Thomas poked his sword in my direction. He waved me closer. "Come here, boy. And kneel."

"I don't know, Mike. . . ." Carly grabbed for my sleeve. I knew she still wasn't sure I could trust him.

But I did trust him. I had a feeling I knew exactly what Sir Thomas wanted to do.

My chest swelled with pride. I went over to the knight. I knelt in front of him.

Sir Thomas raised the sword. He brought it down again, first on my right shoulder. Then on my left. "I, Sir Thomas Barlayne, do dub thee, Sir Michael of the . . . of the . . ." Sir Thomas struggled for the right title.

"How about Sir Michael of History's Mysteries?" I suggested.

"Well said!" Sir Thomas chuckled. "I do dub thee Sir Michael of History's Mysteries."

Sir Thomas stepped back. He held his sword in front of him with both hands. He glanced at Carly. He looked at me. "I will always remember you, my friends," he said. "Now I can rest."

A blue fog rose all around Sir Thomas. It wasn't anything like the purple smoke that smothered Mardren. This was a soft cloud. It hugged Sir Thomas like a favorite blanket. I heard him sigh.

When the cloud blew away, Sir Thomas was gone.

18

"So that's the story. I'm really sorry, Dad. I know how much you wanted a haunted suit of armor. I didn't mean to get rid of the ghost. It just sort of worked out that way."

"That's okay, Mike." Dad ruffled my hair. "I understand what happened. You sure were brave."

Dad put one arm around my shoulders. Carly was standing not too far away. He grabbed her, too. "You, too," he added, laughing. "And just think, all that time we had a wizard in the museum and we didn't even know it."

Carly shivered. "He wasn't a very nice wizard."

"That's for sure." I wanted to shiver, too. But I figured Sir Michael of History's Mysteries would never shiver in public.

Dad grinned. "Wait until I tell Uncle Basil. He's the one who started all this. If he didn't buy Sir Thomas's suit of armor—"

"Mr. Conway!" Someone rapped on the front door and called inside. "Mr. Conway, it's Stanley. From Stanley's Moving and Storage."

Stanley sounded as nervous today as he had the last time he came.

I glanced at Dad. Dad glanced at Carly. Carly stared at me. We all shrugged. Then we raced to the front porch.

When we reached the porch, we all screeched to a stop.

"What is it?" I looked at the huge, wooden crate that Stanley and his helper were lifting out of the van. It had red stamps all over it that said FRAGILE. Stanley and the other guy carried the crate up the front steps. They set it down on the porch. "Who's it from?"

"I don't know." Dad thanked the moving guys. They got back into their van as fast as they could. They were already halfway down Fear Street by the time Dad took out his crowbar.

He worked on the lid, loosening the nails and pushing it up.

Together, we lifted the cover off the crate. The whole box was packed with shredded paper.

"I don't know. . . ." Carly bit her lip. "I don't think

110

I like the looks of this. I'm sure not sticking my hand in there again."

"I don't like the looks of this, either." Dad took a deep breath. "Well, here goes," he said, and stuck his arm into the paper.

I held my breath.

I wondered what we'd see when Dad pulled his arm out again.

Would it be a helmet with fiery eyes peering out from it? Or a magical pendant filled with blue smoke? Or maybe that yucky purple snail, all slimy and smelly?

Dad pulled his hand out. He held a long white envelope.

"What's this?" He frowned and stared at it. "Should we open it?" he asked us.

But before Carly and I could answer, he tore the envelope open. He pulled out a letter and unfolded it. "Looks like a note from your uncle Basil," he said.

"It is?" Carly and I darted forward at the same time. I got to the letter first.

I snatched the letter out of Dad's hands.

"What does it say?" Carly asked.

I looked down at the letter. I cleared my throat. "It says: 'Dear Barnaby, Mike, and Carly. Well, here it is. The armor I promised you. Sorry it took so long to get to you. I don't know if the legend is true, but the old guy who sold it to me says the armor is haunted. I hope so, don't you? See you when I get back.'"

I blinked in surprise. "Does this mean what I think this means?"

"It means . . ." Dad made a face. His glasses jumped up his nose. "I think it means that wherever Sir Thomas's suit of armor came from, it sure didn't come from Uncle Basil."

"Wow!" I flopped down on the edge of the crate.

"Yeah." Dad said. "Wow!"

"Wait, there's more!" Carly pointed at the letter. "There's a P.S. 'Mike, there's something extra special for you in the crate.'"

All the color drained out of Carly's face. "Not another magic pendant!"

We all reached into the crate together. We felt around in the paper.

I found the package first. It was soft. It was wrapped in brown paper.

My heart thumping, I tore off the paper. Some sort of white material. A T-shirt.

I shook it out—and read what it said.

"My uncle went to England, and all I got was this dumb shirt."

About R.L. Stine

R.L. Stine is the best-selling author in America. He has written more than one hundred scary books for young people, all of them bestsellers.

His series include *Fear Street, Ghosts of Fear Street* and the *Fear Street Sagas*.

Bob grew up in Columbus, Ohio. Today he lives in New York City with his wife, Jane, his teenage son, Matt, and his dog, Nadine.

R·L·STINE'S
GHOSTS OF FEAR STREET ®

Is The Roller Coaster Really Haunted?

THE BEAST

❏ 88055-1/$3.99

It Was An Awsome Ride—Through Time!

THE BEAST 2

❏ 52951-X/$3.99

 A MINSTREL® BOOK

Published by Pocket Books